THE
NIGHT
OF MY
HANGING
(AND OTHER SHORT
STORIES)

THE NIGHT OF MY HANGING

OF MY

HANGING

(AND OTHER SHORT STORIES)

KIRBY JONAS

Cover design by Todd Christensen

HOWLING WOLF PUBLISHING
POCATELLO, IDAHO

Howling Wolf Publishing
1611 City Creek Road
Pocatello ID 83204

For more information about Kirby's books, check out:
www.kirbyjonas.com
Facebook, at KirbyJonasauthor
Or email Kirby at: kirby@kirbyjonas.com

Manufactured in the United States of America—One nation, under God
Publication date in electronic format for this edition: May 2015

Jonas, Kirby, 1965—
The Night of My Hanging / by Kirby Jonas.
ISBN: 978-1-891423-18-5

Library of Congress Control Number: 2015916010
To learn more about this book or any other Kirby Jonas book,
email Kirby at kirby@kirbyjonas.com

Dedicated to Todd,
whose genius has led to some of the best
book cover designs I have ever seen

And to men like Jack Schaefer,
Ernest Haycox, Luke Short, and Louis L'Amour,
who were my "pioneers" and blazed the way
for me as a Western storyteller

THE NIGHT OF
MY HANGING

Apologizing don't come easy for me. It never has. That night we fought again, and for me it was one time too many. What I said I said in anger, but I've never been one to say I'm sorry. I walked out of the house, and I never looked back. The thing that hurt worst was seeing my kids standing in the doorway to their room, staring at me with the hurt in their eyes as I slammed the door.

One of the blackest nights I can remember lay like a tarpaulin over our ranch house. I could hardly see our old shed even from ten yards away, and Duke, my buckskin, was a misty ghost in the pasture. Rain pattered like mouse feet on the back of my coat and on the brim of my hat. It touched my face and cooled my anger, but like forged steel it also hardened my resolve. Rachel had hurt me, and I had hurt her in turn. I swore I would never go back to her.

The shed smelled of the hay and straw, must and horse sweat of years. Smelled of oats and molasses and oiled leather. Smelled of the old pine boards that kept the rain off my back for a couple of minutes while I picked up the heavy Cheyenne saddle and horse hair bridle and pulled a Navajo saddle blanket from the rail by the door.

Then once more I walked into the night, my boot soles straining for traction against the mud of the yard. I went between the bars of the gate and spoke Duke's name, and he came to me like the faithful horse he had always been. I saddled him there in the middle of the muddy pasture. Then I rode from there and left the gate hanging open.

On the way into town I had to trust Duke's instinct to find the road. It was so dark it would have given some folks the jeepers, dark like the river bottoms on a moonless night or like the inside of a midnight hayloft full of new summer hay. I was riding hunched in the saddle, hiding my face against the rain, hoping the saloon would still be open in Heron. I had no desire to rustle shelter on a night like this, and I sure didn't intend to ride the whole night soaking wet. Even if Fred Lee was at the saloon, a man I couldn't stand, I had every intention of spending the entire night there in that barroom.

Suddenly, I heard a horse whinny, and my own answered back as he jerked to a stop. I looked up to see a dark shadow through the falling rain, then a flash of light accompanied by an explosion. Somebody had fired a gun—at me! Whoever it was fired once more.

I struggled against my coat to draw my Merwin Hulbert from its holster. I didn't know who I was shooting at, but I knew he was shooting at me. Even if I had been in a good mood that was enough reason to shoot back.

Three times I fired, then four. I couldn't tell if I hit the man. It was so dark, and with the flashes of light from my gun barrel I was soon blinded. But in moments I heard a whinny and the thunder of hooves, and then the road, as far as I could see, was empty again.

I could have gotten off my horse to check the road, to see if I had dropped the stranger from his saddle. But I wasn't about to go lumbering in the dark and the rain looking for a hulk of shadow that might be lying there with a gun cocked and ready. With a curse, I put spurs to Duke, and he galloped off down the road, his hooves making sucking noises in the mud.

It was half an hour before I made out the lights of town through the rain, which now was falling harder and was starting to feel like it had some texture to it. It was cold enough it wouldn't have surprised me to see it turn to snow.

At the Night Tower Saloon I pulled up, soaked and weary and a little scared about my recent encounter. I lashed Duke to the rail there in the rain and left him standing while I climbed onto the soggy porch and shoved inside the big main room, frowsty with the stale odors of alcohol and smoke. There was only one patron in there, a quiet shadow on the far side of the room, slouched over a dark table.

The bartender, to my poor luck, was Fred Lee. Fred and I had decided when I first moved to Heron half a year back that we didn't like each other. He was a man who liked to be in charge, but not the type other folks liked to have lord it over them. He swaggered a lot, threw a lot of knowing comments and lies around. I was sorry to see him there, because I had wanted to tell someone about my encounter on the road, but it wasn't going to be Fred. I'd have to wait until morning and then go hunt up the sheriff.

I ordered a bottle of whisky and a glass and took it to a far corner of the room to nurse it, the opposite corner from the other patron at his lonely table. I had no more than sat down and felt the warmth of the first shot trickling down my throat than I heard a flurry of galloping hoofbeats enter the street. I looked up curiously, pouring my next round as I watched the door to see if the riders would stop here. They sounded to be in a powerful hurry, probably to get out of that miserable mushy rain.

Sure enough, the horses stopped in front, and other than voices in the storm there was no sound for a few moments until boots tromped across the porch and the door slammed open. I was surprised to see three men shoving through the door almost as one, all armed with either rifle or shotgun. I warily lowered my glass as they fanned out from the door, and three more came in between them, scanning the room. All eyes lit on me.

One mustached man with a white hat darkened by rain, its edges glowing a dull yellow in the lamplight, leveled a shotgun straight at me, and I know my jaw dropped. "Get up out of that chair real slow."

I had no words. A man looking down the twin bores of a shotgun finds little to say, at least in those first moments of surprise. In the back of my mind I was aware that some of the men had crossed to Fred Lee, the bartender, but the man in the fore of my mind was this gent in a long, wet duster holding the shotgun at my chest.

"That your buckskin out there?" the man asked. His voice was a course drawl.

"Yeah, sure." My eyes flickered toward the door. Questions were bouncing around inside my head, but I was still too stunned to out with them.

The man's head moved in a slight nod. "Take off your coat, real slow. And take off any guns you're wearin'."

"What's this about?" I finally managed.

"Damnit, move!" His voice had raised. I don't know if he was only mad or if there was fear in that voice, too. It sounded like both.

"All right, I'm movin'," I said. "Take it easy. I'm not lookin' for trouble."

By now several of the other men had formed a half circle around me. Only my back was uncovered by guns, being against the wall.

I was vaguely aware of Fred Lee telling some of the other men that I had just ridden in and that he didn't know me very well. He was telling them I'd always been a surly sort.

I carefully took off my coat and laid it on the table. I took off my gun belt with my left hand and laid it over the top of the coat. My belt knife was hooked on it, and the only thing I had left that could be considered a weapon was a little jackknife in my left pants pocket. Again, with my eyes staring right into the man with the shotgun, I said, "What's goin' on here? Who are you?"

"We're the rest of the boys from the Rafter K, the ones you didn't kill."

I stared hard. My mind raced back. The man in the road! "You talkin' about that fellow out on the road? Hell, he fired first! I was only defending myself."

The shotgun man peered at me queerly, but then his face hardened again. "Get his gun, Luke," he said out of the corner of his mouth. A thin man with wrinkle gashes beneath both cheekbones and a mustache that seemed to cover the lower half of his face came warily around and shucked my gun from the holster. Then he backed away, his own pistol in his fist.

The shotgun man stared me down. "I'm Tick Hollister. Old man Sheets was my boss."

That didn't mean much to me, except that I had heard the name Sheets down at the Cattleman's Saloon. He was one of the more prosperous ranchers around and seemed to be well thought of by locals. Rachel and me hadn't been in Heron long enough to know much about anyone other than some of the folks in town like Fred Lee.

Hollister held his shotgun out to Luke when he got backed up to him. "Here, hold onto this, will yuh?"

Luke just nodded and took the shotgun. He raised it up to his shoulder and trained it on my face. He looked like he was about to shoot a rattlesnake.

Hollister opened up the Merwin Hulbert and peered closer. Then his face hardened, and he looked back up at me, his eyes narrow and full of hate. "There were four shots fired out of a forty-four when Mike Sheets died," he said, talking to the room. "This gent has four spent shells in his gun. And it's a forty-four."

My innards churned. I had never reloaded after exchanging shots with the man in the road! It had been too wet and dark, and I had wanted nothing but to get away from there and get to town.

"I told you, I shot at a man on the road on the way into town. He came out of nowhere and took a couple shots at me."

Hollister scoffed. "My hell, mister! Do we look like a pack of fools? It's darker than the inside of a gut out there. You didn't shoot at no man on no road. Mike Sheets was sittin' at his kitchen table when you shot 'im."

"I'm tellin' you the truth!" I said, my fear making my voice come out sounding hoarse and high. "Yeah, it was dark. He looked like just a shadow, but he shot at me and I shot back."

I glanced quickly around the room, trying to see what lay in all their faces. In a couple of them I thought I might have seen a hint of doubt. Most of them were hard as ice.

"Let's hang 'im now an' be done with it," one younger man said, taking a step forward. "I'll go get a rope."

"I say we get the sheriff an' let him handle this!" one of them said from the back. He sounded almost scared to say the words, so I had a feeling he stood alone in his notions of justice. He pushed his way through to the front. "What if he's tellin' us the truth?"

"He's lyin'!" Hollister snarled. "His story don't add up."

"I seen this man around town," said another man, a pudgy fellow with big dark pockets under his eyes and the ill-matched look of a hardened drover about his build. "He's got 'im a wife an' kids. I'd sure feel better about waitin' for the sheriff, too."

"Sure, Jim. The sheriff's half a day's ride from here!" Luke barked. "What are we waitin' for?"

Hollister was staring at me. He was listening to the others, but I could see the wheels of his mind churning. "You got a wife and young'uns? Where at?"

"South of town," I replied, feeling the first surge of hope I had felt all night. "Rachel's her name."

Hollister's mouth twitched. After studying him and all of those with him I had come to the conclusion that he was the leader of this flock. In the first place, he had to be a good fifteen years older than his nearest contender, and in the second place it was plain they all listened to him and watched to see how he would act. He was the man I would have to convince.

"A lot of killers have wives," Luke growled. "Do we let 'im go because of that? Old Mike had a wife, too."

"Hang 'im!" shouted the man who had been eager to find a rope.

"Simmer down, Cole," Hollister said. "We gotta be sure."

"How?" Cole growled. "Let a court handle it? I've seen the way they handle things!"

"Hush! What time is it? Luke, you got a watch? How long till daylight?"

Luke watched me while he dug inside his coat. His eyes held mine while the shotgun rested across his forearm. He had never bothered to take the hammers off cock, and I half expected to hear it go off. He flicked open the watch and peered at it in the dim light. "It's only a quarter to midnight, Tick. If these clouds hang on it ain't gonna be light for maybe eight hours. What're you figurin' on?"

Hollister looked cross. "I don't know. I think we got our man, but what if we don't? What if Tobe and Jim are right? That's a hell of a load to haul around on your conscience the rest of your life."

"You ain't gonna prove nothin,' Tick," said the hot puncher, Cole. "Any tracks left around the place has sure washed out by now, his or his horse's. That Merwin of his is a forty-four, an' what's more common than a forty-four? That's what a lawyer would argue. We waste time an' let him live till the sheriff gets here he's likely to ride away scot-free. There ain't enough evidence to hold a man on in court. But *we* know the truth!"

I stared at Cole. How could a man be so full of hate? He didn't even know me.

"What if we go look around on the road, see if we can find any sign that he mighta really had a run-in with some stranger?"

Luke jerked his eyes over at him. "You gotta be kiddin', Tick! I'd never call you a fool, but you know there ain't gonna be no sign on the road. Cole's right. The only thing we're gonna get by waitin' around is Mike's killer goin' free. It's pretty dang coincidental four shots was fired into Mike an' now this here galoot has four fired casings in his gun. That's proof enough for me."

Hollister turned suddenly to Fred Lee. "Hey, Fred! Did he tell you when he come in here about havin' a problem on the road with anybody?"

"No way. He came in all surly, got his whisky, and sat down there. He didn't hardly say nothin'."

I could see Tick Hollister's face settling into hard lines as he turned back to face me. I think that was the turning point for him, the point where he made up his mind I was guilty.

"You can't tell me a man would have a fight like that on the road to town an' not come in an' tell nobody about it. That just ain't human nature, bucko. Cole, go get the rope!"

The pudgy-faced puncher, Jim, jumped forward, looking quickly from me to Hollister. "Wait! Let me an' Tobe go ride the road, see if we can find a sign. Maybe he actually hit this other feller. Or maybe he hit his horse an' it's lyin' around there dead. We're all gonna feel pretty sick about this if we find out he wasn't lyin'."

I could see Hollister waver again, and he looked over at Luke. "He's right, Luke. Damnit. I ain't gonna take that one chance away from him. All right, Jim. You an' Tobe, Frank and Cole go ride the road on both sides an' look around. Take some lanterns from the livery with you. We'll look tonight, an' we'll keep lookin' for two hours after daylight. Then if nothin' turns up we take him down by the river and decorate a tree. I'll be damned if I'll let a man kill a boss as fine as Mike Sheets an' then just ride free."

I was still stunned. I stood there cold now on the outside and in, shaking like I had the ague. My breath was coming short, and my heart was pounding fast. I was going to die. They would find nothing on the road. I didn't think I had hit the man, and his horse sure never gave any indication of being hit. I had no more than ten hours to live.

It's funny what goes through a man's head when he knows he going to die. Here I had just had that hellacious fight with Rachel, here I had planned on never going back there, and suddenly I knew that was all I wanted to do. Everything I had in life that mattered was back on that ranch, between Rachel and those three little kids. We had argued, a few too many times, I had been stubborn, and because of that I was here and I was going to die. And Rachel wouldn't even know until it was too late. What was she going to do? How would she make a living out there? Would she have to remarry? Would she have to move herself and the kids to town?

"I've never begged for anything, mister," I said to Hollister when only he and Luke were left standing there. "And I hope you won't consider this beggin' now. But just in case you're wrong, just on that one chance . . . I've gotta see my wife again."

Luke flexed his jaws and spat. He looked over at Hollister. Hollister's face was hard, but in his eyes there was an uncertainty I knew he couldn't shake. It was the one thread of mercy I knew I could count on.

"How do we find her?"

I released a breath. A flicker of hope ran through me from my toes clear up through the top of my hat. I might die, but at least I could tell Rachel some things. I could tell her I was . . . I was sorry. I could even tell her I loved her, and the children too. Half an hour ago that hadn't made one bit of difference to me, but now it meant everything. It was the only important thing in my whole world. Not my pride. Not my stubbornness. Only to let Rachel know I had been wrong. To let her know it for the first time in my mule-headed life.

After Luke left to fetch Rachel, I sat there at that table, staring at the floor, at the tabletop, at my coat, my hat, the ceiling. I looked at everything but Hollister, and he probably thought I was guilty just because I couldn't meet his eyes. But looking at him took Rachel out of my mind, and the kids, and right now they were all I wanted to think of. I didn't want to think of that rope around my neck. I'd seen plenty of men hang, legally and illegally. One way didn't look as painful, but neither way looked pretty.

Luke came back long before the other punchers did. But I didn't think it could be long until dawn. He came back in, and he was alone. My throat seemed to close over. Rachel had refused to come.

Luke looked at me, then finally over at Hollister. His eyes returned to me. "Your wife's outside. She said she wanted a minute to prepare herself."

Rachel appeared in the doorway. She came around the corner of the doorframe with her chin held high, her riding hat and coat all soaked, but her face proud. She looked at me, and her eyes were cool as ice. "Can we talk in private?" she asked Luke.

Luke turned to look at Hollister. After a moment, Hollister said, "Well, I guess we could tie him up somewhere so he couldn't try to get away."

Rachel's attention had turned to the older man. "Are you in charge here?"

"I'm the foreman on the Rafter K, yes. I'm Tick Hollister, ma'am."

I could see Rachel flexing her jaws. She pushed back a strand of her honey-colored hair and took a few steps forward, holding out a steady hand. "I'm Rachel Morgan. Dan is my husband."

Hollister was openly taken aback by Rachel's outstretched hand, but he hastily removed his hat and took it. "Yes, ma'am. I'm sorry about all this, but . . . everything looks pretty plain."

"You've made a mistake, Mr. Hollister. I promise you my husband would never kill anyone. Not unless they tried to kill him first." Her face and her voice were both as cool as could be.

"Yes, ma'am," Hollister replied, dropping his hand away and swiping at his mustache. "Luke, get some piggin strings, would you? Tie his hands up."

"I got no piggin strings."

"Well . . ." Hollister looked around helplessly, avoiding Rachel's eyes. Finally, he met her steady gaze. "Ma'am, I'm afraid we can't leave you alone with your husband if we can't find some way to secure him."

"Then it must be that way," she said instantly.

From across the room I heard something slide across the bar top, and I looked over to see Fred Lee with his hand on a shotgun lying on its side with its barrels pointed toward me.

"I'll make sure he don't leave, boys. If that counts with you."

"Shotgun counts for a lot." Hollister looked over at me. "You an' the barkeep friends?"

"Not hardly," I replied.

"I can't stand the man," Fred put in. "I'm just tryin' to help out. And I don't ever miss anything I shoot at, neither."

Hollister looked at Luke, as if for approval, and Luke just shrugged. Hollister looked around the room, toward the door, then around the room again. It was obvious he didn't want to go outside.

"There's my bedroom right there," Fred said, pointing to a door at the far end of the bar. "You can sit in there while you wait if you want."

Hollister nodded thanks, and the two of them went and disappeared behind that door. The room fell silent. The man at the other table had long since left in the excitement, and that left only me, Rachel, and Fred.

Rachel sat down across from me. Her eyes searched mine, and I could see no vestige of anger in hers. But I didn't know what she was looking for, and with her eyes on me this way I didn't know if I could still say what I wanted to. But I had to force myself to say it. For Rachel's coming here had changed nothing with these hard cowpunchers. In a few hours I would be dead—a cottonwood blossom, to be blunt.

I felt my hand reaching across the table as if it had a mind of its own. It lay across Rachel's hand that rested on the table. She met my eyes, and mine held. Knowing I would soon be dead gave me a strength in my words that I had never known. "I've always been stupid, Rachel. But I've always loved you. I couldn't ever say it. I've always loved you. I always will love you. I'm sorry. I can never tell you how sorry I am for everything."

Rachel was strong, and I was so proud of her. I saw her chest rise with a deep breath, and for a moment I saw her eyes glitter. Then she looked away, her jaw clamped. She didn't speak, but I understood.

She pulled her hand away and got up, pacing the floor. She came back and sat down, staring at the top of the table. But me, I stared at Rachel. I wanted to keep every detail of her in my brain. I wanted her to be the last thing in my thoughts when my horse went out from under me.

"Who's with the children?"

Rachel didn't raise her eyes. "They left one of the cowboys there. They were all asleep. They cried themselves to sleep after you left."

"Jack will be strong for you, Rachel. He'll be a man for you. Stand by him while he fights with this. Let him work it through. He'll think the world took his pa away."

Again, she just flexed her jaws. She looked up, then quickly back down.

We sat there for what seemed an eternity. Every time I looked at Fred he was staring at me over the top of that shotgun, that smug look on his face, his lips smirking beneath his bristly brown mustache.

I saw daylight begin to creep into the room, a diffused, gray daylight coming through clouds that probably would not let this day see the sun. I was still wet, and it was deathly cold in the room. My feet were numb, my mind too. I heard a lone horse gallop down the street and stop in front.

Soon, Cole came inside. He looked around, surprised, then looked over at Fred. Fred jerked his thumb. "They're in there." Cole went into Fred's bedroom and shut the door.

Rachel suddenly got up and went to the door, walking right in. When she came back out she was holding her chin high again, her cheeks white. Instead of walking to my table, she walked to the window, and putting her fingers up on the sill she stared out.

My throat ached dully like my chest. My whole body was numb, perhaps more with fear than with the cold. Finally, I stood up and walked toward her. I stopped at her left shoulder.

"They've scoured the road with lanterns and torches," she

said, not even turning to look at me. "They found no evidence of what you told them."

I had no answer. I grimaced, turned and went back to the table. I sat down and for the first time since the cowboys had shown up I downed a glass of whisky and poured another, staring at it there on the table before me.

An hour later, another horse came in. The man came through the door, and it was the man I assumed to be Frank, who I had never heard speak that night. He gave me a hard, hateful look across the room, and that said all I needed to hear from him. After getting the word from Fred, he also went to the bedroom and disappeared.

The next half hour dragged by. Rachel wouldn't come back to the table. She wouldn't even look at me. Her face was as unmoved as a dead woman's. She just stared out the window, and once in a while she would remove her hat and brush aimlessly at it, straighten her hair a little and put the hat back on her head.

I sat at the table and felt the noose tighten around my neck. I kept my poker face intact as well, but with every moment I could feel my life slipping away. Images kept coming to my mind, images I had to throw away. Jack, Alyssa, little Danny. Their faces kept coming to me, smiling at me sometimes, sad others. At last I let them come to me and stay, because I knew I would never see them in real life again. These punchers would not wait that long, and they would not let that kind of emotion enter into the job they figured they were chosen to perform. If they saw my children later they could feel sad for them, but they wouldn't take the chance of their sad faces clouding their judgment now.

I would never see my kids again.

I bit my lip and took another swallow of whisky, thinking about that big year-old stud running with the wild herd that I had been wanting to catch and geld for my own remuda. The spring on the south side of the property was looking like a fountain last I checked it, and the herd on that side was sleek and healthy going into winter. I had a saddle sitting in the shed that

I had wanted to repair for . . . Jack. A young, strong, stubborn face like his father's jumped into my mind, and I clung to it for a moment, then took another swig of whisky. I grimaced, looked down at my shaking hands.

The light coming through the window was not sunlight, but it was the kind of light you know comes from a sun hiding only behind clouds, not one hiding below the horizon. And then I heard the sound of two horses plodding quietly. That would be Jim and Tobe.

I got up woodenly and walked the length of the room to Rachel, where she was staring out the window, fidgeting with her reticule. Through the raindrops on the window I could see a dusting of white on the mountains, but none had stayed on the street. It was just a mass of mud. Tobe and Jim were walking their horses, and they drew in at the hitch racks in front of the saloon. They looked at each other and then glanced up to see us staring at them. Both of them looked quickly away. They got off their horses, and Tobe came up onto the porch, then paused to wait for Jim, who was fussing with his cinch. Tobe said something, and Jim looked up at him, then came up onto the porch slowly, forcing himself not to look our way. They came inside, and both glanced toward us, then scanned the room.

Their faces were confused. "Where're the others?" Tobe asked.

"In my room," Fred replied smugly. "Don't worry." He gave the shotgun a couple of taps. "I've been watchin' the killer."

Jim frowned, and he and Tobe walked toward the door.

I hurriedly looked back at Rachel. She was frowning too, tugging at a loose thread in one seam of her reticule.

I placed shaky hands on both of Rachel's shoulders, and she turned around. She still didn't look up at me. "I have to make the most of this. You know this is the last time we'll ever see each other."

A picture of the times we'd shared together, of the children who had come to grace our home, of the land we'd cleared together came running into my head, and for the first time in many minutes our eyes met, and both of us had to fight back the tears. I was losing my Rachel, my children, my everything. How was she going to live? I had ruined her life. Mine didn't matter. She would have to stay here and fight for her every meal, for her dignity, for her soul. What had I done? God, what had I done?

Tears trickled down my cheeks, and Rachel fell into my arms. Her breathing told me she was doing everything she could not to break down. She was clutching me around the middle like she meant to break my ribs.

The door opened across the room, and all was silent, but then one set of boots tromped across the floor and out the door, and once he was outside I saw the wearer of them was Cole. He went to tug a coiled rope off his saddle, his face grim.

Someone walked over and stood beside us for a moment, and then I heard Tick Hollister's voice. "Sorry, ma'am. But we've gotta go. Best you stay here."

Only a man who is about to be executed could ever know what was going through my head. I was going to show these men how strong I could be. I believed in God, and he was going to be there waiting for me, knowing innocent blood had been shed. My stomach was only filled with sick fear for those I left behind.

Hollister and Luke grasped me by the arms, and it took two of the others to pry Rachel away. I heard her finally start to sob as we cleared the front door.

The sun was streaming light through one tiny hole in the clouds when we stepped onto the soggy porch, and that one ray of light was for me.

We heard a wagon splashing up the road at a good clip, and when it came into view I saw one of my neighbors driving it, a man named Jeb Peters. He saw us and hit his horses with the ribbons, making one more burst of speed before he pulled up in front of the saloon.

"Somebody help me get this gent out of the back of my wag-on! He's shot up."

Peters jumped down and splashed around the wagon through the mud, letting down the tailgate of his wagon. Jim and Tobe and Frank followed him to the wagon while the rest of us looked on, Cole with the lasso poised in his fist.

They all looked into the back of the wagon, then back at us. "Tick, get over here!" Jim yelled.

Hollister let go of my arm and hurried down the steps. He got to the back of the wagon and looked in at what the rest of us couldn't see. Cole had followed them too, and it was just me and Luke alone on the porch now.

Peters looked over and happened to notice me, and he waved a preoccupied greeting. "Howdy, Dan."

Then he returned his eyes to Hollister, who looked up. "He's dead," Hollister said.

Peters nodded. "Well, I didn't figure he'd make it all the way to town. He was bleedin' bad. Out of his mind, he was. He kept talkin' about some old man he had to kill. An' some feller he ran into on the dark road that shot him for no reason. Didn't make no sense."

Hollister's face had gone white, and he looked up at me. I was standing alone on the porch because Luke had stepped away from me and also stood staring dumbly at the wagon bed. Fred Lee was standing in the street, and when he turned and stumbled past me back into the saloon he wouldn't meet my eyes.

I heard my woman sobbing then, and I turned and looked into her eyes. She was standing on the porch and staring at me. She tilted her head to one side. When she threw up her arms to come to me it was like she had been holding my life there, and she offered it back to me. I took her against my chest, and we both cried while I whispered how I loved her. I didn't care who heard.

JUSTICE FOR
DALLAS FORD

Dallas Ford took charge of the posse because Sheriff Briggs was laid up with a broken leg.

And because he was Dallas Ford.

Old Tim Nettles was riding home with a five thousand dollar payroll in his saddlebag when the highwayman stopped him on the highway near Blackrock Canyon. Nettles had been a tough man in his younger days. In his own right, he still was tough. But he was pushing eighty now, and although he still had the metal to run a 3,000 acre ranch and a crew of rowdy cowboys, he didn't have the speed or the strength to fight the young man who sat tall and broad in the saddle and spoke with a voice of iron.

Nettles knew when he handed over the saddlebags that it was going to be many a hard month before he saw that kind of money again. And there was no way he was going to pay off his cowboys. That hurt Nettles most of all, because those boys had broken their backs for him bringing some of that rough stock out of the rugged mountain country on the backside of the Portneuf Range. But the boys would stick by him. They always had. Those boys rode for the brand.

The fact was, when Dallas Ford stood in the bed of his wagon and cried out for volunteers for a posse, the boys from Tim Nettles's LN Ranch were first in line. Of course it was in part because they wanted to be paid. But it was also because the boys from the LN Ranch thought the world of Tim Nettles, and they weren't going to let him lose everything he had worked so hard for when he bought the dregs of the Hamilton Ranch after Seth Hamilton died and left his wife to sell off his holdings.

Old Tim Nettles stood by at the back of the crowd and watched the anger seething in his neighbor, Dallas Ford, and in the cowboys who worked his own ranch. Worry clouded his face.

There were twenty men in the posse when Dallas Ford tallied them. Twenty tough men with sand in their craw and a bent to see justice done. But to some of them justice meant bringing the robber in alive. That wasn't what Dallas Ford thought of as justice.

"Ford, what do you plan on doin' with this feller when we catch him?"

Noah Roberson, although he was not one of the ranchers, was a no-nonsense, upstanding man who believed in justice and hated to see a good man like Nettles wronged.

"You saw what happened last time," said Ford curtly. He and Noah had had differences of opinion before, and he seemed to expect one now. "The man that stole those cattle over by Preston walked away with a fine. He's probably rustlin' stock in Wyoming now. I know what you're thinkin', Roberson. Bring him back to the sheriff. Well I'm in charge of this posse."

Others brought up similar concerns. They all wanted to see how far Dallas Ford intended to go, for there had been talk around town that Dallas Ford meant to make an example of the next criminal who crossed his path. Of course no one hinted that they thought Ford would commit murder, and Ford was vague in his answers, but several of the men who had originally appeared to be ready to join the posse suddenly found other matters to tend to.

Finally, old Tim Nettles himself raised his voice, and the crowd quieted. "Dallas, I sure appreciate all your concern for me. But I have some other concerns of my own. You know Henry Briggs would bring this boy in alive, sure as you're standing up there. I know you mean well, but if it comes to it it isn't our place to take a man's life. You don't ever know what led him to have to rob me."

Dallas Ford smirked. "That's just like you, Tim. It almost sounds like you're feelin' sorry for this fella that held a gun on you and could have killed you."

"That's just it, Dallas. He didn't kill me!"

Big Dallas Ford wiped a callused, deeply veined hand across his blond mustache. "It's but a matter of time, my old friend."

When Dallas Ford had jumped down out of the wagon and climbed onto his bay horse, he looked around and saw two of his hands standing at the edge of the porch of the Pacific Hotel. "What are you boys doin'? You have leave to come with us."

The two hands shot each other worried glances. One of them, Chet Hankins, cleared his throat. "Well, boss, we'd sort of like to not go."

"What are you talkin' about?" Ford barked. "I'm ordering you to go."

The other hand, who went by the name of Boots, turned a paler shade of gray. "We can't go. I— I'm tellin' you, boss, you don't really wanna go, and we can't go either."

Dallas Ford turned to the others and waved them on. "You boys head toward McCammon. I'll catch up."

He climbed down from his stocky bay and walked toward the two hands, his batwing chaps flapping against his boots. Coming to a stop in front of Boots and Hankins, he hooked his thumbs behind his belt. Even his thumbs were muscular.

"I'm tellin' you boys for the last time you'll go with us. Or you'll provide a real good excuse why not."

Hankins held up a hand as if he thought a blow was forthcoming from his boss. His eyes were full of fear, and for a moment he struggled to speak. "Boss, don't make us go. I wished I could ask you to stay here, too. I surely wish I could."

Ford looked back and forth at the two men for several seconds, his eyes hard and veiled. "When I get home we'll talk about whether you boys will still be workin' for me or not. I don't know if you're yellow, but it's sure looking that way. When Nick gets back from Raft River, you tell him he's in charge till I get back. I guess if you boys break your backs while I'm gone you may still have a job."

Nick Ford was Dallas's only boy. Dallas had been giving him more and more responsibility on the ranch in the past year, and he hoped it taught him a little responsibility too. His only wish was that he could have been on this posse, too. It would have been the perfect opportunity to see what kind of a man he was. Ford secretly hoped when his son returned he would try to catch up to the posse and show the whole town of Pocatello that none of the Fords would shirk their duty.

Dallas Ford caught his twenty men at the edge of town and led them off toward Blackrock. And Tim Nettles stood in the street of Pocatello staring after them and wishing Sheriff Briggs hadn't broken his leg falling off his horse two weeks before. Dallas Ford was going to make bad things worse.

The going was fast at first, for the robber had made no attempt to hide his trail. He was riding a fast horse, and he rode it hard, not sparing it in the up-hunched sagebrush hills crowding Blackrock Canyon. For half a day they saw nothing but deer and an occasional elk. Once they startled a black bear, and some of the cowboys took shots at it until Dallas Ford swore at them and told them they would warn the robber they were coming.

It was early in the afternoon, after they had all climbed back in the saddle from letting their horses graze and blow a while, that Dallas Ford came right out and revealed his intentions. "We're going to kill the man that robbed Tim Nettles," he swore to Jud Cleef. "He only robbed a man this time, but it was an old man that everybody thinks well of. And next time who knows if he'll stop at just robbin'. One time somebody will decide to fight him and he'll have to kill. But when this trip is over he won't have a chance."

Someone overheard Ford's statement, and word spread through the posse as word always does. Those at the head of the posse rode for a couple of hours with pursed lips. After making his intentions plain, Dallas Ford settled in to studying the trail, fingering his rifle butt, and riding.

Jud Cleef, Andy Nichols, and Fred Hawley, all riding close by him, rode with concerned faces they couldn't hide. The only talk was far back at the rear of the posse. Three men in the middle of the posse had for the past hour slowly let themselves drift to the rear of it. They hovered farther and farther back in the dust.

When Dallas Ford called a stop to rest in a stand of junipers he noticed a missing buckskin horse. He took a toll of his posse, and now there were seventeen. The buckskin was gone, as was a sorrel and a bay. Dobkins, Mendez and Freily.

Ford was quiet for a long time while some of the men dozed in the shade of the junipers. It wasn't until one of the cowboys said something about the three missing riders that Dallas showed he knew they were gone.

"Some men ain't got the backbone to do what needs to be done. We're better off without 'em."

Noah Roberson wiped a gloved hand across his lips, then pinched them with his fingers to clean off the dried saliva and dust. Roberson was fifty-five years old, and he had seen his share of mob rule. He had left the responsibility of his Pocatello dry goods store to his eighteen-year-old daughter in order to come along on this posse, and now he made it plain why.

"Dallas, I'm concerned about the outcome of this chase. We're coming up fast on statehood here in Idaho. The governor is not going to be pleased if he hears a mob rode off and killed some man when he's hoping for the job of governor of the state himself. It just won't look good. This fellow can be brought in alive as well as dead."

Dallas stared at Roberson through hooded eyes the entire time he was talking. He chewed on a tiny branch of juniper and bided his time to speak, then made sure anyone close by heard him.

"Noah, I'll make no secret of the fact that I think you're a coward. And I'll make no secret of the fact that I think you're a fool. The way our court system has turned in the past couple of years there's a good chance this feller will walk out of there just like the other one did.

"And if he hid the money under some rock they won't touch him and he'll go off, free to spend it, while one of the best friends a community could have sets there five thousand dollars poorer. I don't really want you on this posse, Noah. I never did. But if you stay you will do what I tell you, and you won't interfere."

Noah had sat up straighter. He was by far the smaller of the two, but he met Ford's eyes squarely. "And what if I do?"

"I'll kill you."

The silence was thick enough to plant corn in. Finally, Noah Roberson stood up. "Well, sounds like to me you're just itching to kill. Period. Take a warning, Ford: I'll take a sight of killing. If we're going to catch the man that robbed Tim, I would suggest we go."

"We'll go when I'm ready." It made sense to be riding, but it was plain that Dallas Ford wanted to say when.

Roberson walked over and tightened the cinch on his chestnut. Six of the other townsmen sheepishly got up and followed suit. When they mounted and rode out after the robber, Dallas Ford didn't even favor them with a glance. He just kept looking down his back trail and chewing on his juniper branch until well after the sounds of their passage faded. Finally he stood up and stretched.

"All right, boys. Let's go."

The day was hot and muggy, and a dark bank of clouds loomed in the west. The smell of sagebrush and dried grass and juniper lent a tangy edge to the dusty smell in the air. Of course there was also the smell of horse sweat and saddle leather, and the occasional pungently sweet odor of fresh crushed horse droppings.

Half an hour later they caught up to Noah Roberson, who sat his chestnut on the side of the trail. The six who had ridden out with him were not there. Dallas looked around nonchalantly and studied the trees. He saw no one but Roberson. He was curious where the others were, but he was too furious with Roberson to ask. He was glad when Jud Cleef did.

"They're gone," said Roberson with a shrug, and he pointed up a side canyon. They cut through there to miss you boys."

"Miss us?" Ford's face darkened.

"They had enough."

Dallas Ford blew a breath of disdain out his nostrils and swung his eyes around the eleven men left. "We'll weed all the cowards out of this bunch yet." His eyes swung meaningfully over Noah Roberson as he nudged his bay into motion on the robber's trail, still plain in the dust among the sage.

Since they had had a late start out of town, they had to make camp less than twenty miles out of Pocatello. They threw their blankets down among the sagebrush and prepared to shiver all night. No one had brought more than one blanket, not wanting to weigh their horses down for a ride that could conceivably last for days.

The stars sprinkled like a sprawling city across the sky. The clouds had all gone, and the midnight dome was as clear as spring water. All around them coyotes made a strange music until the throaty cries of a wolf pack silenced them. Crickets chirped, and wind rustled in the summer leaves of rocky mountain maple. Even the cool air seemed to have a scent all its own.

When dawn came there were five riders, Jud Cleef, Andy Nichols, Fred Hawley, Noah Roberson and Dallas Ford. Every one of Tim Nettles' ranch hands had ridden out.

This time Ford was furious. He couldn't believe that they had escaped without his detecting them. It was that which made him angriest of all. He threw camp goods around the sage for a while, kicked a few rocks and flung more cuss words than a crew of cowboys learning to read.

Jud Cleef finally admitted to hearing the others go. When Ford berated him and asked him for more information, he glanced over at Andy Nichols, who by the guilty look on his face had also known.

"I heard Bawdy asking the other hands what they were going to do when they caught up to the robber. He kept asking if there wasn't some way they could let him live. He was worried about killing a man that might surrender and beg for his life. He got the others worked up enough that they all decided none of them wanted to hear him scream for his life. They all figured one Dallas Ford was enough to bring this man down."

This seemed to placate Ford, who stopped throwing and kicking things and just mumbled under his breath while he saddled up his horse. He didn't say anything to the others as they rode out. Relief filled their faces.

It was along about noon when Fred Hawley started realizing how bad his backside hurt. He wasn't a cowboy or a soldier, he was the owner of a hotel. He felt sorry for Tim Nettles, sure, but this was turning out to be far more than he had bargained for. Dallas Ford was a harsh taskmaster, and the sun was baking his brain inside his black derby. Wasn't there any end to this trail?

He stared at the back of Dallas Ford's head. He looked at the other riders, all of whom rode silently, with sagging shoulders. A look of vast relief came over his face when Andy Nichols called for a rest. They all climbed down and stretched their legs. Fred Hawley's face began to sweat more heavily. His glance flickered up to Dallas Ford, then to Nichols, Cleef and Roberson. Finally, he spoke softly to Roberson.

"You don't really think he'll kill that feller when he catches up, do you?"

"He's talked too much not to," Roberson replied under his breath. "I'm going to try and stop him, but I might need your help."

Hawley swallowed hard. "Stop him? What do you plan to do?"

"It depends on what he does. I plan on doing whatever it takes."

"Even … *kill* him?"

"Fred, he plans to kill that man in cold blood, whether he

surrenders or not. That man could have killed Tim Nettles, but he didn't. I think he deserves a trial. What if we're on the trail of the wrong man? What if he has a family dying of some disease and he's just trying to get money for a doctor? We don't know all of the story. I don't want a human life on my conscience."

Hawley stared at him, sweat dripping off his chin. "You'll have Dallas Ford on your conscience if you kill him to stop it."

"I've yet to be convinced he's human."

When Hawley turned away from Roberson, his hands were shaking, and there was sweat in his eyes. He wiped it away with a fumbling sleeve. With a deep breath, he reached into his vest pocket and pulled out a little jackknife. He bent down and coaxed his horse to raise its foot as if to check it, and with one more courage-building breath he sank the knife blade an inch into the soft frog of the horse's hoof.

Hawley's horse gave a grunt and jerked its hoof away, making him drop the knife. Trying to seem calm, but shaking like a rain-drenched possum, Hawley reached down and retrieved the knife and slid it into his pocket. When he looked over, Andy Nichols was watching him. Nichols quickly glanced away.

When they had taken a breather, everyone mounted back up and started on. They hadn't made it a mile before Fred Hawley mopped his brow with a sleeve, then called out. "Hold up. I think my horse is goin' lame."

Andy Nichols turned to look at him, and they shared a guilty glance. Dallas Ford jogged his horse back to Hawley, looking Hawley's animal up and down. "Walk him a ways. Let me look."

Tossing a worried glance at Nichols, Hawley walked the bay out a ways from Dallas Ford. When the big man swore, he turned around with concern in his eyes. But Ford was looking up the trail.

"Well," Andy Nichols spoke first. "He sure can't keep riding that horse the way it's walking. Maybe the rest of us better head back to town. We can wire ahead for the law in the next town to be on the watch." Nichols's eyes were hopeful.

"No!" Ford boomed. "We won't let him go." He sat for a long, thoughtful moment. No one else seemed to dare speak.

Finally, Andy Nichols said, "I'll just let Fred ride back with me on my horse. We'll get another horse and come back." By the way his eyes darted about, it was plain he had no intention of returning.

"Go on and run then, you worthless coward. Tim Nettles never hurt nobody, and you're willing to let his robber go unpunished."

"You know, Dallas," Jud Cleef spoke up. "Tim Nettles doesn't want you to kill this fellow. He wants him brought back in alive."

"To these teary-eyed courts? Not on your life!" Ford growled. "Are you turnin' yellow too?"

"I'm not yellow, Dallas." Cleef straightened up in his saddle. "I'm being sensible, and you're not."

"Well, the whole pack of you can go back." Ford turned to glare along the trail he meant to continue traveling. He didn't meet anyone's glance, which didn't matter since no one else was looking at him.

"All of you get. I'll take this man alone."

Jud Cleef's face was red, but when he looked at the others it was with eyes full of more relief than shame. He started to turn his horse, but Noah Roberson was in his way. When Hawley climbed off his lame horse and up behind Nichols, Noah Roberson pushed his mount past them and up alongside Dallas Ford. His back was straight as a preacher's wife, and his jaw was set hard. Dallas Ford didn't even look at him. He just spurred his animal on.

They were jogging their horses way too often for Noah Roberson's taste. Three hours had passed since the others turned back, and they had jogged five times as much as they had walked. The robber never had made any attempt at hiding his sign, seeming totally oblivious to the fact that he might not get away with his crime. But for some time now he had been circling back around toward the road that led to Malad and Salt

Lake City, and if he made that road it would be nearly impossible to tell his sign from any other on the road. Without Ford saying it, Roberson knew that was why he pushed his mount so hard.

They rode up on a sagebrush-covered hill covered with stumps where the railroad had clear-cut for ties. The Oregon Shortline ran along below them. They could see its silver rails shining in the sun, not far from the Portneuf River. In the distance they could see a tiny object bouncing up and down, and Dallas Ford pulled out his field glasses. Noah Roberson watched him expectantly, then frowned when he put the binoculars away. Ford kicked his horse and rode down the hill.

An hour later the last of the twilight was fading away, and Ford and Roberson sat their horses in the gloom, the tang of dust and horse sweat in their nostrils. They didn't talk. They were still too mad at each other. They looked about them as both wondered what they should do, and how they should proceed from there. Then, like a beacon in the night, a fire appeared a few hundred yards away. Dallas Ford's eyes sprang to life, and he pulled out his rifle.

Roberson spurred up alongside him and grabbed his arm, which Dallas instantly wrenched away. "Don't kill him, Ford. Don't kill him. I swear the courts aren't as bad as you say. Give him a chance to explain."

Ford stared his scorn at the smaller man. "To all those bleeding hearts back in town? No thanks. He'll pay the way all criminals should."

"I won't let you do it!" Roberson cried out.

Without warning, Dallas Ford swung with his rifle in just one hand. Its heavy barrel collided with the side of Roberson's head, stunning him. He fell limply over the back of his horse, which bolted and jogged away a few yards before turning to look back. With one glance down at Roberson, Ford caught up to the other horse and reached down to gather its reins. Roberson was a coward, but of course he wouldn't leave him horseless out here. Still, he had to make sure he couldn't interfere again until the affair was over.

Only a hundred yards out from the campfire's glow, Ford climbed down and tied both of the horses in the thick willows along the river. Then, leaving his rifle in the scabbard, he drew his Colt .45 and crept forward on foot. He approached the bandit from the rear. The man was sitting there so bold, silhouetted in the campfire light. A criminal who might not have paid, except for the no-nonsense justice of Dallas Ford.

Ford didn't even call out. He gave no warning at all. He could see just enough to make out the saddlebags across the man's lap, and he could see him thumbing through wads of bills and throwing them down on the blanket at his feet one at a time. He stalked to within fifteen feet and raised his pistol.

And then Dallas Ford heard a voice yell out behind him, the voice of Noah Roberson. "Ford, no!"

Ford's heart leaped. He had just turned back toward the sound of the voice, but his instincts made him whirl back. The man at the fire was spinning around, and Dallas heard a shot. He was vaguely aware that it zipped past him in the dark, and in that moment he fired his own Colt, once, then again.

With a little cry and an arch of his back, the robber fell backward onto his blanket. Dallas Ford swallowed the only touch of doubt he had felt since hearing Tim Nettles's story in town, and then he walked forward. He was going to make sure of this man before Noah Roberson ever reached the camp.

The firelight made an eerie mask of the man's face. Dallas Ford looked down at it out of morbid curiosity to see the man he had made sure would rob no more. The man was young, clean-shaven. He was, in fact, not much more than a boy. The firelight played a weird pattern across the face, distorting it, but...

Perhaps it was Dallas Ford's mind not wanting to see what lay before him. Or perhaps it was truly that the firelight battling against the darkness had changed the face enough that for a moment he didn't recognize it. But when at last he did, Dallas

Ford's knees buckled, and he fell straight down on them, not feeling the rocks on which he landed. He grabbed the man's shirtfront and jerked him up, peering into his face, speechless. His mouth was open as if he had been struck a blow, which, in a sense, he had.

For long minutes, until most men's arms would have failed, Ford held up the body. The body of his son, Nick Ford. He stared into his lifeless face. At last he managed to choke out a cry, more animal than human, and he let go of his son and fumbled for the pistol he had dropped in the dirt beside him.

A few hundred yards away across the sagebrush Noah Roberson heard a single, sharp crack.

THE WIND

It haunted Ben Harper like a tormented demon. Howling with inanimate hate, it tore at his clothes, his hair, his face, and drove tiny bullets of sand and gravel at him without mercy until he almost hoped for death.

It was a sure thing he couldn't win this fight; he could not kill the wind.

For days on end it had cried, whined, moaned along the bob-wire fence. It picked at him when he ventured out for fuel or food, taunted him by forcing its little drifts of dust underneath the cabin door when he tried to hide. His horse was gone. The wind had driven him down the trail back the way they came. The few surviving cattle were gone, too. Numbly they had walked, disappearing with their rumps to him, away from the wind that drove them—and him—mad.

He took up an old pad of paper and a blunt pencil. Tried to draw pictures of horses, of houses, of people. But always the wind conquered, and he was left pacing, listening though he dared not hear, watching for he knew not what.

Somehow he managed to unearth the bag of tobacco he hadn't been able to dig up three days earlier. Like an old locomotive he began to smoke, lining up the little stubs of cigarettes as he smoked them down to the smallest possible stub, standing them on end along the blunted, broken end of the pine table. Soon there were seven smoke stubs there in a perfectly arranged line—and no tobacco left in his sack. And the wind still drove into his life, hungry, insatiable. Where that wind came from waited the devil.

Back in New York it should be like spring. Tulips, daffodils, violets should be in bloom. Lilacs and dogwoods and fruit trees would soon be in full flower, and when the welcoming sun didn't shine, a gentle mist would fall. Here in Wyoming it was only the wind in the sage, in the bobwire, in the eaves. Down in the canyon it would rage as hard, tearing and grasping at the aged cottonwoods until they, like Ben Harper, would beg for death. But death would not come.

This was how it ended, that awful winter of 1887, the winter that had driven the stock to madness, piled them up like cordwood along miles of fence. The cattle had begged for relief, and they had found it—in death. They had died, some eighty percent of them, it was estimated, and then, like some sick joke, the snows had all melted and the sun had burned the grass-less plains to dust.

The cattle had suffered death, in the snow, but now, in the dust and the gale-force wind, Ben Harper was suffering life. Here he was, ten miles from the home ranch, and the only song he had heard in days was one written by banshees.

Harper stared at the empty plate on the table. It was graced by a shard of bone, the only sign that nourishment had ever existed in this cabin. The meat was gone, the flour was gone, the coffee was gone. Even his ammunition was gone, and between him and starvation was a ten-mile walk in boots made only for riding.

He stared at the bone, dazed. With his hair disheveled and his face gone ash-gray, he looked dead already. Yet the miserable shaking of his body showed he still clung to life. And then, as if coming from a trance, he began to hear it. The stillness, the deadly silence of the world.

Somehow the wind had ceased.

Ben Harper pitched his chair backward like a madman and stumbled for the door, flinging it open to stare around him, bewildered. The world was brown, the dust still hanging defiant in the breathless air. The mountains were only a dull brown shadow against the lighter brown of the sky. Even the horse shed was a dull gray hulk without detail.

Ben Harper immediately regretted the passage of the wind. With it being gone the stench of death came back to settle over the line camp—the death of God only knew how many Hanging D cows. Hanging D. Harper didn't want to laugh, but he did. The "D" that was hanging so pert from that crescent was supposed to stand for his Scottish boss's last name: Duncan. But to Ben Harper it stood for something else: death. The Hanging Death Ranch. And yes, with the departure of the savage wind the stench of awful death hung in the brown air like a pall.

There was a faint stir, a tinge, of blue in the western sky. With the desperate hope it lent his weary body, Harper lunged back into the cabin and clutched his holstered Colt from its hook beside the door. He started walking as he buckled it around his waist, his eyes fixed toward the north, toward the Hanging D's home spread. He laughed again when he felt the hardness of the Colt high against his hip. Lying to himself that he was out of ammunition had kept him, for the last twelve hours, from going out to try and squander his one last bullet on hapless game to fill his stomach. He had promised to keep that last round in case the wind never ceased—for himself...

D O N ' T
FALL IN LOVE
IN ABILENE

He could love her, or he could hate her, but one thing was certain: Abilene, Kansas, would never be denied a man's attention.

Like a jumble of colored blocks, there she lay on the horizon, among the dust, the acres of stockyards, and the waving yellow grass. She was the blood and the guts, the bone and muscle of the cattle industry in 1871.

The end of the trail.

"There she is, boys. Straight ahead. That's Abilene."

Jordan Farley spoke with a voice as dry and dusty as the twelve miles of Kansas topsoil he and his Texas trail crew had looked through, breathed and chewed on since five o'clock that sultry August morning. He dragged off his broad-brimmed, once-white plantation hat and wiped at the mud encrusted on his brow. The heavy dust coated every inch of him and his horse, from his faded blue bib-front shirt to his eyebrows and brittle dark mustache. It filled his ears, his nostrils, wriggled past his parched lips to form a permanent grit between his teeth. He felt sorry for his drag riders; he recalled those days at the rear of the herd all too well.

Jordan Farley's thirty-fourth year had slithered up on him on the trail like a rattler on a kangaroo rat. None of his crew would have known it at all, except the cook, an old friend, had seen fit to make him a birthday cake their third week out of Fort Worth.

The cook kept a shard of mirror in the chuck wagon, and

Farley stole a glance in it before retiring to his bedroll the night of his birthday. The years had not been his friend. Wrinkles creased his face, cracked the sun-blackened skin alongside his sky-blue eyes, dug washes alongside his mouth. And the dancing cook fire accentuated these signs of age.

But he didn't care anymore. His beautiful Marie and their two small children lay in the ground ten miles outside Fort Worth, victims of a range fire that had swept away his home and his life two years ago. His dreams and hopes had died with them, along with his will to participate in society.

"Think we'll git t' see the town t'night?" queried "Jingle" Braden, the tow-headed seventeen-year-old mounted beside him.

The skin around Farley's eyes creased as he glanced at the youth, who had never been up the trail. "I promised you would, son. But it'll wait till we've bedded down the cows." There weren't really any cows in the herd of two thousand steers, but in cowboy lingo "cows" covered all creatures bovine.

Fernando Gutierrez, the swarthy, mustached rider on Farley's left, had rolled himself a quirley and touched a match to its twisted end. Smoke curled out between his lips, and he squinted past Farley and the acrid smoke at Jingle, a broad smile breaking through his thatch of black-whiskers. "You jus' might not like what you fin' there, *amigo*. The *señoritas* in this town, they are very wicked." He laughed and winked at Farley, who cast him a preoccupied glance.

Yet Jordan Farley only feigned this preoccupation. Fact was, those *señoritas* Fernando mocked filled his mind to overflowing. They had since… heck, he couldn't remember when. Days, anyway. But not for the same reasons his crew dreamed of them.

No, to Jordan Farley those ladies of "questionable virtue" presented only a threat. A threat to the memory of his lovely Marie. And a threat, also, to the boys who had come up the trail with him, loyal hands he had come to feel about almost like he would his own sons. He felt that way at the end of every drive.

But of course they weren't his sons, and he couldn't hold them back. Three dusty months they had waited for their night on the town, and they had earned it. And exactly what had they earned? The chance to throw away their money and their innocence.

A hundred yards back the way they had come rose a hideous moaning of sore, tired bovine voices accentuated by a rumble like distant, constant thunder. Farley turned and squinted over his shoulder. Through the pall of dust, he could only clearly see the first forty or so Rocking Arrow steers, coming on in pairs, and his two point riders beside the lead steers.

The two cowboys came on doggedly, their horses plodding, but the slump-shouldered, weary posture of the last several days had changed. Now they sat taller in the saddle, their shoulders squared, their necks craned as if that would better help them see the country ahead. He had told them they were close to the rail-head. Tonight the whisky would flow, and so would the love—or some base semblance of it.

At Jordan Farley's orders, his punchers, except for the two unlucky souls who had drawn night guard, gathered around the chuck wagon an hour before sundown. They shifted their attention back and forth anxiously between their trail boss and the not-so-distant ramble of buildings and stockyards called Abilene.

Farley didn't smile as he gave his last bit of advice and guidance to his boys. Anxiety drew his heart up too tight in his chest for him to smile. In a few minutes, these trail-weary riders would descend on Abilene and be on their own. It was more like Abilene was going to descend on them. Only five of them had ever witnessed firsthand the wickedness of this or any other cowtown. He wished he could somehow protect them.

"This town's full of wolves, boys, and don't you laugh at me. Ask Cholla, there, and Boots." He nodded toward two of the riders who had made this trip before. "Ask Fernando. Let your guard down and some ace will slip inside and take you for all you have. It ain't just the men, either. In fact, I'm more worried about the women. And I purposely didn't say 'ladies.' There ain't any ladies in the side of town where you'll do your whoopin'. The only side you're allowed on.

"And another thing. Wild Bill Hickock's runnin' this town, and he's trigger-happy. He's quick to shoot, and I hope you'll all stay clear of him. There's plenty more like him, too. Gamblers, toughs, killers. I know you boys are proud of them shootin' irons, but here's my advice to you. If you ain't got it on, you can't pull it, and most men won't call you out unless you're heeled. I'd suggest you leave the guns here in the chuck wagon. Let's keep Wild Bill as calm as we can so one of you don't get shot. Chances are good there's a law against carrying guns anyway. Most of these towns have enacted laws like that the past couple of years."

The glances of the punchers flickered around at each other, each wondering if his partners would heed the advice. Finally, Cholla, Boots, and Fernando began to peel off their gun belts, and Farley cast them a grateful glance. When the younger crowd saw the seasoned hands shedding their weapons, most of them did, too. Only three kept them on, and these made a point of not meeting Farley's gaze.

"I think you're makin' a wise move, boys," nodded Farley at the others as he wiped his mustache with the web of his hand. "Now back to the women of Abilene. You'll be in the red light district, and ladies don't go there. I wish you boys could just suddenly know about women. If you did, you probably wouldn't even go on into this town.

"But I remember bein' wild and wooly like you, and times ain't changed much. You've got your wild oats to sow. But just promise me this: you won't let the wool get pulled over your eyes. The women you'll meet are a hardened bunch. Some'll show it right out, so even you slick-ears'll have no doubt.

"But there's them that know better how to play the game, and they'll croon and make eyes and say pretty things. They'll do anything to make you think they want your heart, but it's only your wallet they want. Just don't be fooled. You'll end up with a broken heart, and I ain't playin' mama to you all the way back to Fort Worth, listenin' to you cry about love gone bad.

"You go have your drinks and enjoy your women, and waste all your hard-earned cash on gamblin'. You'll hate yourself later, but kids always gotta learn the hard way. Just remember two things: don't get yourself in any scrapes you can't get out of with talk…

"And don't fall in love in Abilene."

A general rush for the horses ensued when Farley gave the nod, and even though Jingle Braden reached his mount among the first, he only took the reins and didn't instantly fling himself into the saddle. Fernando Gutierrez reined his buckskin around in a circle, smiling broadly at Jingle and waving his hat about in the air. "Come on, Jingle, let's hit the bathhouse. *Amigo,* you stink!"

Jingle gave a laugh and waved Fernando on, and the Mexican winked and let out a *whoop*, clamping his hat back on and charging after the departing riders. Farley glanced at Jingle as he walked over leading his horse.

"Would it be all right if I just hang around with you for a while, Mr. Farley? You know yer way around better'n the rest of 'em." Even though Jingle had known Jordan Farley for three years, he still called him mister. It was the rare man Farley allowed to call him by his first name, and since Marie there hadn't been one woman he had allowed that familiarity. Not a single one. And he doubted he ever would again.

Farley nodded. "Sure, son. I'd be happy to have you."

Jingle smiled broadly and swung into his saddle, waiting for Farley, who had to *crawl* into his. He wasn't a kid anymore. Farley turned and waved to the cook, and he and Jingle cantered off toward town.

By the time they left the bathhouse, the other hands had long since disappeared into the crowded guts of Abilene. Farley and Jingle both wore new duds, procured at one of the general stores that remained open until later in the evening when trail drive season rolled around. Of the ragged outfits they had worn into town, only their boots, hats, and vests remained, for a man didn't easily give those up. Especially the boots. No drover with any pride would buy a pair of boots not made special for his feet. That was below their standards. And all trail hands, unless some drastic accident had done their boots in on the trail, wore Texas boots.

As they walked down the street, Farley gazed toward the orderly side of town Abilene's citizens had put off limits to cowboys. Children played there, he guessed, and ladies in pretty dresses strolled the quiet streets beside their men.

Farley knew he should be there, too, not over here where the wild ones caroused. He didn't like the style over here. Never had. Quality of life and life itself meant very little in the red light district, at least to a truly Christian man. And Farley didn't think this side of town even knew what the word "love" implied.

But because of his occupation, the town's "decent" citizens had banished him to roam the bawdy streets and frequent the brothels, saloons, and gambling houses of the wild side of town. Truth be known, he'd have been over here on the wild side anyway, because he had to keep his boys in check and out of trouble. Even at trail's end, he couldn't relinquish the notion these boys were his own.

But he still longed to be on the "proper" side of town, where the people were honorable, good, and clean, and where he could get a glimpse now and then of a child who still possessed innocence.

Farley and Jingle stopped at a gambling house to waste a few dollars "bucking the tiger" at the faro table. Then they lost a few hands of poker, spent a dollar on drinks, and moved on.

Darkness had fallen across the town, and merriment rattled the windows of every saloon and gambling hall, but the Red Dog hummed more quietly than the rest. Farley and Jingle stopped in front of it and looked up and down the lamp-lit street at the carousers. With a shake of his head, Farley led the way inside the saloon, and they weaved their way to the bar.

A bartender in a greasy apron finished setting a jar of pickles on top of the bar and wiped his hands, then his huge handle-bar mustache with one of those big hands. He looked at Jingle, then Farley, and his eyes settled on the latter. "Howdy, stranger. What'll it be?"

"A root beer," said Farley. He figured to let Jingle make his own choices, but the new hand seemed more than happy to follow his lead, and he asked for the same. Mildly amused by the requests, the bartender *plunked* chunks of ice into two huge mugs and filled them to the brim with root beer.

Farley threw two bits on the counter to pay for both. To Farley's surprise, they found an empty table at the back of the room, and they sat down to observe the crowd. Wide-eyed, Jingle watched and listened to the sounds of celebrating and said very little. By now, he realized Farley didn't really want to talk, anyway.

Jordan Farley raised his eyes just as she walked into the room.

Rouge didn't mar her cheeks, nor eye shadow darken her eyelids the way it did most of the women on this side of town. The hem of her light green calico gown hung lower than most— past her calves—and the bodice rode higher, revealing no cleav-age line. She wore a simple locket at her throat—a gold heart.

Farley didn't mean to stare, but for some reason he did, and Jingle noticed it and glanced over at the woman, too. Farley gripped his drink in his hand and wondered what it was about this woman. What set her apart from the rest? She had to be a hard one, or she wouldn't work here, but something about her was different.

Strain had played a big part in her life; Farley had a habit of reading people, and this stood out like the smoking brass lamp hanging from the ceiling in the center of the room. Something about her mouth and eyes revealed this strain—a hardness yet a sadness, a weary, bedraggled stare.

As for physical appearance, the woman didn't shine in the crowd, but he wouldn't have called her homely. Out of the braids piled on top of her head, drab brown wisps curled down to hang limp against a neck lined with two even creases deepened by the yellow smear of the lamps. Her unpainted lips turned down slightly at the edges, but sometime in the past they had seen laughter, judging by the wrinkles outside them, and the lamplight belied a certain softness there.

Though tending toward fullness of figure, little fat marred the woman's frame, and her hands, while not big, were not dainty, either. They had seen their share of work, and not much of it pouring drinks, Farley guessed. She was a quietly attractive woman, he admitted, though that admission grated on him. But he could never say more for her. She had condemned herself when she set foot inside the saloon.

When their eyes chanced to meet across the crowded room, Farley's held. He didn't want her to see him looking, but something about her wouldn't let him look away.

Her frank gaze appraised him, then rested on his eyes, and he caught a faint flicker of recognition. The look vanished, but she seemed to have made a decision about him. She stepped away from the back doorway and moved toward his table.

Farley watched her for a moment longer before his better senses took over, and then he looked away, squinting across the room through the tobacco smoke and taking a long sip of his root beer.

Even the inexperienced Jingle Braden had caught something in Farley's glance, and he looked from the woman to his boss as she tentatively approached the table, jostled and pawed at now and then by the punchers she passed and managed to sidestep.

She stopped before them, and her fingertips rested on the smooth pine slat tabletop. Though Farley had initiated her decision to approach the table, she looked at Jingle as she spoke. "Mind if I sit down? It looks like the only peaceful place in here."

Jingle glanced over at Farley, his face reddening, and shrugged nervously. "Why, uh… Sure, ma'am." He waved toward a chair. The woman looked over at Farley and stood watching him expectantly, making no move to take hold of the chair. Jingle glanced again at Farley, then cleared his throat. "Oh, sorry, ma'am." Jumping up, he grabbed the back of the chair and pulled it out for her.

The woman's gaze held on Farley for a few moments, then fell away to Jingle. "Thank you. You're a gentleman." Her eyes flashed toward Farley as she said that, but she didn't look directly at him.

Jingle pushed the chair back in as the woman sat down. Clearing his throat again and glancing nervously at his root beer, he eased back onto his own seat, scooting the chair around as if he couldn't find the right position for it.

Farley's eyes crinkled as he watched the youth's discomfiture, and in spite of himself he looked over at the woman to catch her reaction. Her eyes stared between the two of them, though she seemed aware of the boy's discomfort. Her lips had turned up at the corners, like Farley's, and when her eyes swung into the older man's, a glow lit them vaguely, like the sheen of newly polished leather.

They were brown eyes. Not deep brown, but more golden brown, the irises surrounded by darker rings and flecked here and there with umber specks. They swam with curiosity, with friendliness… and they were framed by loneliness. But without loose invitation, Farley decided. Just a warm welcome saying she would listen with rapt attention to anything he said. Because of his lost Marie, he found the feeling disturbing.

"My name is Martina Singleton. People here call me Martie." The soft words came as if answering a question, as Martie's eyes glided from Farley to Jingle and back. She massaged the jewelless fingers of her left hand with her right ones, and looked down at them for several seconds before bringing her eyes back to meet Farley's.

Farley didn't complete his part of the name exchange, just nodded. Martie tried but failed to hide the hurt in her eyes, and it shamed Farley inexplicably. But he didn't plan to ever meet this woman again. What need did she have of his name?

"I'm Jim Braden," Jingle broke the silence when Farley didn't seem willing to respond. "They call me Jingle, on account of my spurs. This is my trail boss, Mr. Jordan Farley. We just brought a herd up from Fort Worth, Texas."

Red-faced, he shot a look at Farley, as if for his approval, and Farley just nodded again, a mere dip of his chin. But secretly he was glad Jingle had spoken for him. It gave him an unforeseen, unexplained pleasure to have this woman hear his name spoken, and he tried to shake the sentiment away and stared off again at the bar crowd.

Although Jingle and the woman both had opened the way to be referred to on a first name basis, Farley had no intention of it. She knew his name. That was enough. If ever a woman called him by his first name again, it certainly wouldn't be a woman like this. People might hear and think him a man of loose morals—morals like Martie's.

Martie just nodded, looking at Farley as if expecting him to speak, then dropped her eyes again to her hands. Her lips parted as if to say something, but she remained silent, glancing over either shoulder as if seeking a way to excuse herself.

Farley avoided speaking to the saloon girl. Even though she seemed different than most of them, she was still a loose woman, or she wouldn't work here. As such he would rather not let himself be drawn into conversation with her, and he refused to spend any money on her. Let her go to another table to earn her keep. Marie's spirit could be very near him now, and he wouldn't disgrace her memory by lowering himself to buy this woman a drink, although she almost certainly expected it of him. After all, it was her occupation to get men to buy her drinks.

Even as he thought this, Farley found his eyes on her again, wondering. She didn't fit in, not in this crowd. The lack of makeup, the modest dress, the quiet eyes and voice. Was she new? Untrained? Or just lazy? Was she just a low class hooker with a crib out back, or did her entertainment stop at conversation and a dance? He had met some of that brand, but they were scarce as crickets at a bonfire.

The uncomfortable silence dragged on between the three of them until the strain wore on Jingle. He cleared his throat again as he set his root beer down and glanced cautiously at the woman, whose eyes at the moment studied Farley's face. "Been any excitement in town?"

Startled by the voice, even though only a small sound in the general din of the room, Martie pivoted her eyes to Jingle. She made sort of a shrug with her hands and face and drew in a breath, letting it out as a soft sigh. "Oh, just the normal. Wild Bill came in three nights ago and found some fellow in here who'd been talking bad about him, supposedly. He buffaloed him with his pistol and dragged him off to jail on some charge or other."

Farley's bored eyes perused the room while Jingle and Martie warmed up to each other and began to converse in earnest. But somehow his gaze kept turning back to this woman at the table before him. It wasn't her showiness that drew him, but her lack of it. He had to keep forcing his eyes away, trying to think of Marie. But Marie wanted to fade out of his memory like she never had before, and he found himself having to make a conscious effort to bring her back to the surface. He hated that most of all.

Farley was watching Martie when Jingle made one of his quiet-humored jokes. A spontaneous laugh tinkled in her throat like crystal, and like a splash of mountain morning sunlight her face lit up, driving from it any plainness Farley might have thought he saw. Her perfect teeth sparkled dully in the lamplight, and her nose wrinkled up at the bridge, but it was the warm brown of her eyes that tugged Farley into her soul. They met his at precisely that moment, and this time they held while her smile gradually— very gradually—faded away, leaving her lips parted. But the smile faded away only from her lips. It remained in her eyes.

Farley, catching himself smiling at her, swung his eyes away and wiped brusquely at his mustache, drawing the upward curve of his lips back down. He looked up just in time to see a middle-aged, dark-haired man in a gray suit stop beside the table, glancing at them all, but last and longest at Martie.

"I see you're not drinking tonight, Martie. Maybe you need to mingle with the crowd a little more." His eyes held a subtle warning as they swung back to Farley, then once more rested on Martie.

Martie forced a smile, her face flushing as she looked from Jingle to Farley with faint supplication in her eyes. "Jim Braden, Jordan Farley, this is Mr. Brood. He owns the Red Dog. Well…" She looked again at Farley and Jingle as she placed the palms of her hands on the table top in preparation to push herself up but hoping someone would stop her. Farley swung his eyes away to the crowd, and Martie's fell with an almost audible crash.

"Wait."

Jingle's voice broke the tension as Martie rose halfway out of her chair. He looked for Farley to back him up, but when Farley just stared back the boy's face settled into new lines of resolve. "What'll you have to drink, Martie?"

Martie smiled and relaxed again into her chair, flicking her eyes up at Brood. They shone with moisture when Farley glanced at her. Jingle had saved her from the saloon crowd. "I'll have a sherry," she said. "With ice."

Brood looked grudgingly at Jingle, then at Farley. When Jingle started to rise, Brood motioned him back down. "Sit tight, son. I'll bring it out. It'll be four bits."

He held out his hand, in which Jingle deposited six bits. "The change is for the lady," the boy said haltingly. The businessman handed him an appraising glance and then waded off through the crowd toward the back of the bar.

After Brood had departed, the silence rang at the table for a full minute. Then Martie's sherry came back, and she held the glass between both hands and stared into its depths. At last, she raised her eyes, and Farley felt her stare and met it.

"You don't like me," Martie said. Her voice held no emotion, but sadness filled her eyes. "You don't remember me at all, do you?"

Farley stared at her, then shook his head. "Remember you. Should I?"

"You helped me once, in San Antonio. I was in the train depot with no money. Someone had stolen my purse. You bought me train fare to Topeka. You had a woman with you then—your wife, I think. A beautiful blond woman. Very, very beautiful. And a little baby boy with the bluest eyes."

Farley felt like a fool, and he started to nod again. "Yes, I do remember you now. Sorry. I see a lot of faces."

Martie pursed her lips and dropped her eyes, shrugging. "Oh, don't fret about it. With a woman that pretty on your arm, I wouldn't expect you to notice a face like mine."

A sudden, uncharacteristic urge welled up inside Farley to tell her she was wrong. He was no mind reader, but she plainly needed a compliment right then. *You're a very pretty woman. You just need to find yourself a new calling.* That was what he wanted to tell her, but he didn't. Once a saloon girl, always a saloon girl, and he had no interest in her beyond a passingly pleasant glance now and then.

Brushing off her self-deprecatory comment, Farley asked, "So what happened to Topeka? I thought your family was there."

Martie sighed. "They're gone. The fever had taken them before I got home. Only graves were left."

On a whim, she took the heart-shaped locket from around her neck and clicked it open, revealing a photograph of a bearded man and woman with two girls. "That's my mother and father," she revealed. "And my sister Elaine. The other girl is me."

Guilt washed over Farley as he looked politely at the picture, but he brushed it off. He wouldn't excuse his judgments of this woman. Even though Martie had lost her family and had nothing, there were other ways a woman could make a living. She could have found something better for herself than saloon work. Even as he thought this, he found himself staring at her picture. What would his daughter have looked like at that age?

"What about your wife and son? Are there other children now? Waiting for you in Fort Worth?" Martie asked.

Jingle dropped his eyes from Farley's face, looking down at his root beer. Farley drew a deep breath and glanced around the room, wiping at a crumb on the tabletop. He didn't meet Martie's eyes.

"I had a daughter since I met you in San Antone. They're all dead now, too. Range fire."

"Oh, I'm so sorry." Martie made a move with her hand as if to place it over Farley's, then as quickly withdrew it. She looked down and rolled her sherry glass between the palms of her hands, watching the ice sparkle with lamplight as it danced on tiny waves in her glass. Then she looked back up, meeting Farley's dully gazing eyes. "I never meant to bring up that kind of hurt. Please forgive me."

Farley shrugged. "I'm sorry, too. We both lost loved ones."

He looked away, clenching his jaw and swallowing a lump in his throat. Moisture drained into his eyes, but he blinked it away, aware of Martie's eyes on him. He saw her reach across the table again, hesitantly, then felt her soft hand close over the top of his with a gentle squeeze. It was warm. Incredibly warm. His instant reaction was to jerk his away, but for some reason he didn't. For some reason he left his hand in the center of the table, feeling Martie's warmth course through his veins.

Then he looked over at her, and their eyes locked and held.

A string of shots suddenly crackled from somewhere down the street, and Farley's heart jumped inside him as he retracted his hand. It wasn't uncommon to hear shooting in the streets of Abilene, but every time Farley heard it he wondered if it didn't involve his boys. He still had a responsibility toward them, at least till they left this town.

Most of the shooting in cattle towns was out of pure drunken celebration, not violence. But this time a cry rose up in the street and carried down past the Red Dog Saloon, and as word flew Farley learned a Mexican drover had been gunned down.

With his heart in his throat, he excused himself and left the saloon, headed toward the edge of the red light district, where the shooting was supposed to have taken place. Jingle followed him, almost running to keep up, and they left Martie standing on the porch, watching anxiously after them. They hadn't gone more than a hundred yards when she stepped away from the saloon doors, drawing a light blue knit shawl about her shoulders, and hurried after them.

When they reached the invisible dividing line between the "good" side of town and the "bad," Farley had to fight his way through a throng of drunk, yelling cowboys, saloon girls, gamblers, and buffalo hunters. A man with long hair, an aquiline nose, and two ivory handled Colt Navies thrust behind a flowing red sash stood at the edge of the crowd, holding them at bay with a sawed-off shotgun.

Farley had seen Wild Bill Hickock before, but he would have known him from his description anyway. He glanced past him where several people knelt beside a man prone on the ground.

"Marshal," Farley accosted Hickock, walking close in spite of the shotgun's threat. "I'm Jordan Farley, trail boss for the Rocking Arrow ranch, out of Fort Worth. They tell me a Mexican drover was shot down. Can I see him and make sure he's not one of mine?"

Hickock jerked his head toward the fallen man. "Go ahead. Make it quick and then return to your side of the line."

Farley nodded thanks, and then he and Jingle almost ran to those who knelt beside the victim. Farley shouldered his way in just as a man in a black three-piece suit stood up away from the body. He heard someone say the word "dead" just as his eyes fell upon the lifeless face of Fernando Gutierrez.

As quickly as he recognized Gutierrez, Farley turned away and pushed Jingle back. "It's Fernando, kid. He's gone."

Farley walked back to Hickock, who had just been joined by a group of deputy marshals, all armed with shotguns or rifles. When Hickock looked at him questioningly, he said, "Marshal, that's my man. What happened?"

"A mix-up between cowboys and some buffalo hunters. If those are your boys, maybe you'd better come with me. They headed into the wrong side of town to hunt down the man that did the shooting. Maybe you'll have more luck talking them into putting down their guns than I would."

Farley concurred then turned to Jingle. "You stay here, Jingle. Just stay put. Damn it, I told those boys to leave the guns!"

Even as he spoke, his eyes fell upon one of the hands who had insisted on retaining his pistol. Now his holster was empty. Another one of the holdouts stood beside him, and his holster held no weapon, either. Confused, Farley looked from their holsters to their faces.

"Who's over there? Where's your guns?"

"It's Boots and Cholla," said one of them. "They made us give 'em our guns."

Farley's heart fell, and he swore. "All right," he yelled at them. "Get any of the hands you c'n find an' get back to the herd. All of you!"

"You coming, mister?" Farley heard Hickock's voice above the din.

He turned to face the marshal. "I'm ready."

"Not quite," said Hickock, scanning him. He held the sawed-off shotgun out to him. "You might need this."

Yeah, to protect myself against you, Farley thought wryly.

"What about you?" he queried. Hickock was now the only one with no long arm.

The lawman just gave Farley a hard look, touching a finger to the butt of his right pistol. "I think I can handle myself."

They started off down the dusty street, Farley cursing the water wagon that had fallen down on the job. He'd had enough dust for the last three months; he didn't need it in town, too.

"All right, boys!" Hickock's authoritative voice carried down the street. "We're coming to take you in, so you'd best throw down your guns and come scratching the sky."

No one answered, so the marshal split his men up, sending them down side streets. Farley stayed by Hickock as he continued down the main street, but now and then he drifted off to check other areas. He kept watching Hickock. The man was tensed like spring steel, his hands empty but poised very near his gun butts. He was a showy one, all right. And he must be as fast as they said, to have given up the assurance of the shotgun. Either that, or he was just a fool.

When at last they heard shooting, it came from back toward the red light district, and they turned and made their way toward the sound at a fast walk.

A man appeared around the corner of a house, holding a pistol down against the side of his leg. In the fleeting second it took to recognize Cholla Varden, Farley saw the twin Colt .36's coming free in Hickock's hands. He yelled out.

"No!"

Farley recognized his own voice as he tried to tell Hickock this was one of his men. He didn't hear the shot from Hickock's gun, but he felt an insistent pressure against his right side and felt himself jerked sideways. He looked at Hickock, who by this time had recognized him and stared, his lips clamped tight.

Numbly, Farley walked past Hickock toward Cholla Varden, still holding the shotgun Wild Bill had pressed on him. Blood streamed down the side of his vest, but he didn't even seem to notice it as he saw Boots Henry round the corner, his hands held high in the air.

Cholla dropped his pistol to the ground and raised his own hands, staring from Farley's wound to Hickock. By the look on his and Boots's faces, they knew the lawman held their lives in his hands. The deputies rushed past Farley, taking Boots and Cholla ungently in hand and leading them away. One of them brushed against Farley as he passed, and Farley's knees folded, sending him to his side at the corner of the house.

Hickock looked around him as the crowd gathered, Jingle at its forefront. Three well-dressed women, presumably upstanding ladies of Abilene, stood nearby, staring in horror at the bloody scene, their hands to their mouths. Neither they nor their husbands, nor any of the citizens of that side of town offered aid as Jingle knelt helplessly beside his boss. A couple of cowboys who didn't even ride for the Rocking Arrow stepped in to lend assistance, but none of them knew what to do, and their hands were rough, in spite of their good intentions.

Jingle, almost in tears, looked up pleadingly at Hickock. "Why'd you shoot him, Marshal?"

"When I turned around he looked like he was trying to shoot me. He shouldn't have yelled," Hickock said brusquely. "He was carryin' a gun," he growled to excuse his actions.

The crowd had parted moments before, and Martina Singleton stood staring at Wild Bill Hickock. "Yes, he was carrying a gun," she said. "Your gun."

She walked over and knelt down in the blood beside Jordan Farley, prying the shotgun from his grasp and throwing it in the dust at Hickock's feet. Without a word, the marshal bent over and picked up the shotgun, then stalked off after his deputies.

Martie turned and started to unbutton Farley's vest, then his shirt. He looked up at her and smiled into her warm eyes, feeling weak, partly from loss of blood, and partly from feeling those hands undress him, then knead around his wound.

He opened his mouth to speak, but Martie put the backs of her fingers to his lips to silence him. "You can talk later, Mr. Farley."

He smiled weakly, watching her gentle face as she removed his bandanna and pressed it against his wound, stanching the flow of blood.

"You're going to be all right after some rest, Mr. Farley. I'll have them carry you to my cottage. I'll sleep on the divan," she added, her face coloring.

Farley looked up at her, then smiled lopsidedly. She smiled back, and it lit her face up like an angel's, which he guessed she was. His guardian angel. He was suddenly glad to have to recuperate here in Abilene. It would give him a chance to see more of this girl. To figure her out. To thank her.

He raised his head weakly and looked into her eyes. "You can call me Jordan," he whispered.

THE GRAVE OF
INDIAN BILL

Days like these, when I was alone, my heart still throbbed.

The chill in the air, the bracing smell of pine and fir and mahogany on the wind, the sound of gravel snapping from the frozen mud of the trail—all of it brought slamming back to me the day I said good-bye to Indian Bill.

Morning frost still glittered on the autumn grass when I saddled my red roan gelding and rode away from the ramshackle ranch house. I took the trail south, winding through patches of broken granite boulders and gnarled aspen trees as we climbed ever upward toward the jagged skyline.

I splashed across Tower Creek, its waters crackling over the rocks, its flow diminished now that most of the snows were gone from the high country and nights were freezing hard so what was left couldn't melt. My horse grunted with exertion, bunching his hindquarters to propel us up the slope toward the sawtoothed ridge. We had left the timber now; on this side of the hill it was too cold and windy and the soil too poor for most trees to take hold. But far up the slope towered one lonesome old fir tree, its gray, furrowed trunk whipped and battered and bent by the wind. A lone branch curved away from the rest of the limbs as if grasping for someone in one last futile plea for help. Toward this lonely tree I pointed the nose of the roan.

A year and a half gone I had ridden out of this valley I called home, right after spring roundup. Not by choice, but because there was nothing left here for me. Things change beyond a man's control, and a smart man can see when he no longer belongs. I knew that then, and I still knew it today. I knew it when I said goodbye to my friend, Indian Bill, and sent him on to his reward. But on this day, two years since we parted, I felt myself drawn again to this place, this narrow, lonesome valley, this country known only to the elk and the deer and the wolf once fall roundup carried the cattle and range horses down to the lowlands. I had to visit my friend. I needed to try once more to understand the cruel ways of man.

I stopped the roan a hundred yards from the old fir, dismounted, and led him the rest of the way, my heart aching. There beneath the shelter of this tree, among the waving yellow grass, hunched a pile of stones—cold granite chunks wrenched by the elements from the ridgeline above. I had placed those stones there myself. I had put them there to cover my friend, Indian Bill.

I plunked down near the grave, tugging off my hat to wipe sweat off my forehead and cheeks before it could turn into balls of ice. The roan stood nearby blowing, catching his breath, and each time he exhaled, a great silvery gust of steam puffed into the air and was stolen away by the wind.

I replaced my hat and stuffed my gloved hands inside my coat, staring out across the narrow valley and the great spired mountains beyond. This had been Indian Bill's home. It was fitting his life should end here and he should have this magnificent view of the snow-dotted peaks that towered on and on to an eternal horizon.

William BlueHorse was a half-breed Shoshone. His mother was Redbird, cousin of the great Chief Washakie. His father, Daniel Riggs, had come from northern Maine in fifty-nine. He'd come looking to escape the strife in the east, to avoid the great season of war chiseled on the future annals of the land. I had heard he was an honorable man, but there were those who argued that point. They said he lost all honor when he took an Indian woman to wife.

William BlueHorse, once Billy Riggs, had grown up in the

mountains. He learned young the ways of his mother's people, and his father encouraged his association with them, hoping he wouldn't learn the avarice and petty hatreds of his own people. Bill learned to live with nature, to take from it only for survival, in a spirit of kinship, and to give back at least as much as he took. At the age of twelve, he set out alone into the mountains to become a man. Before his lonely vigil ended, he had a vision, a vision of a great blue horse with lightning in its mane and eyes in which he could envision his future. He dreamed he tamed this horse and rode it throughout the land, doing good to others. Thus he earned the name BlueHorse, through his mother's people. When his father died in an avalanche two years later, he took the moniker permanently, and the name Riggs became only a reminder of the kind, loving man who fathered and raised him.

Even though William's father was a white man, to folks back then if a man was half Indian, he was *all* Indian, or maybe worse. And as for Bill, on top of the fact that he had black hair, dark skin and eyes, like a Shoshone, he had chosen to live like one. So to most of the white folks thereabouts, he was just that. A Shoshone. And I remember early on they took to calling him Indian Bill. But Bill didn't mind the nickname. He was proud of his heritage. And most folks that called him that said it in a friendly way, for in spite of the few with an unquenchable hatred for any Indian, Bill was well-liked in those parts.

I remember the time Bill saved young Seth Horton from a grizzly bear. Seth was a white boy, and the whole town toasted Bill that day. Another time he rode all night to rescue the school-marm, Mrs. Aimee Sharp, from a blinding snow storm that had led her astray on the way home from school one afternoon. He wouldn't even take credit for that. He claimed Mrs. Sharp was intelligent enough to find her own way home and would have reached it eventually anyway.

Indian Bill was somewhat of a local celebrity. He wore his jet-black hair short—shorter than many white men, and except for his customary buckskin shirt, he dressed like a white man, too. But otherwise, he looked the part of his Indian forebears. He had high, sharp cheekbones and wide, finely formed lips and sparsely whiskered cheeks. His nose was pointed like the eagles he so admired, and his eyes were a deep, deep brown, and set back beneath arched brows.

No matter how Bill dressed, he was a physically appealing presence from an early age. I remember many times watching him and seeing the women of our town turn and stare, whispering and giggling. Some of them were even brazen enough to whisper their thoughts to me, knowing I was his friend and word would probably get back to Bill.

Standing six-foot-four, with broad shoulders and a broom handle-straight back, Bill had the lithe, graceful movement of a deer. He could dance with the best, the white man's way *or* the Shoshones', and many a heart was broken by him at church socials and barn raising parties. There were plenty of women who'd have run off with Bill, but he never found the one he wanted. He remained a bachelor until the day he died—a warm, caring man, but a loner.

Boys for miles around idolized Bill, not only for his good looks and easy manner, but because he had mastered the skills most boys dreamed of. He could shatter a pine cone at a hundred yards three shots out of five and he could rope and ride any wild horse that was ever brought to him. On that score, Bill just didn't "break" a horse, either. Bill *tamed* his horses. He treated them like friends, and they grew to trust him—even to love him, if a horse feels such an emotion. His horses were more like dogs than they were horses, always kicking up their heels and champing at the bit when he came out to ride.

Anyway, Bill was quite a hero, to the ladies and to the kids. And even though I heard many a slighting comment about him from certain of the menfolk, I always figured most of it was out of pure jealousy. And that was too bad, because Indian Bill was probably the gentlest man I ever knew, and the easiest to like. A man must really have had to fight his heart not to like him. I never saw him do one spiteful thing. He was always the first to help a lady across the street, to give anything he had to help a friend—or even a stranger. But of course to Bill, everyone was a friend, even those who talked badly about him behind his back—well, most of them, anyway.

One day I had ridden into town for supplies. I tied my horse and packhorse in front of the dry goods store and walked in, and Bill was standing there. A grin flashed across his face, and he stepped to me in three long strides.

"Hi, Tom!" he beamed. He stuck out his hand and shook mine heartily. "Hey, I was just talking about you."

I laughed. "Oh yeah? I thought we agreed you were going to stop that."

Bill laughed with glee and jerked a thumb toward the clerk. "We was discussing yer liking of peppermint candy. Fact is—" he reached into his coat pocket and withdrew two long sticks of it "—I was just fixing to head out to yer place an' bring you this. You'll need it soon. Roundup's about coming, ain't it?"

"You didn't have to do that, Bill," I said with a smile. "But it sure is mighty kind of you. Yeah, roundup is comin' right up. I was headed over in the morning, in fact. I just stopped in to get some supplies laid by."

Bill shoved the peppermint sticks closer with a grin. "Well, take 'em then. And let's go make yer order." I took the candy, and he threw an arm around my shoulders and steered me over to the counter.

After I had ordered my goods and Bill and I had loaded them onto my packsaddle, he offered to buy me dinner down at the cafe, and I accepted. I hadn't had a meal besides those I cooked myself in a good three weeks, and a man can get pretty tired of his own cooking, especially if he cooks like I do. They say it's impossible, but many's the time I've tried to boil water and just burned it to a crisp.

On the way over to the cafe, I saw the Murphy brothers, Si and Dick, swaggering toward us. Si, the mustached older brother, wore a pair of woolly angora chaps and a big Colt Peacemaker strapped on his right hip. Dick wore a Montana Peak cowboy hat, gauntlets and a piebald calf hide vest. They weren't neither one of them as dandy as those get-ups might make them sound, though. Fact is, back in the nineties, them angoras and a pinto vest were right popular.

I sighed when I saw the Murphys, having no desire to run into them today. I didn't have any particular problem with them myself, but they didn't treat Bill good. Besides, they knew Bill and I were friends, and I had started to feel a chill in the air in the last few months whenever I met them. They and Bill had some argument at the spring roundup, and the Murphys never forgave a grudge.

I caught the exact moment when Dick noticed us coming toward them, for his eyes went flat and mean, and he turned and slapped Si on the shoulder, making some remark I didn't catch at the distance. The Murphys were already between us and the cafe, and even though I could have crossed the street on pretense of other business, my stubborn streak made me walk straight ahead. I knew Bill wouldn't have walked away, anyhow.

"Hey, it's the Injun," Si sneered, thirty feet away. "What brings you into town, Billy Boy?"

I glanced at Bill, who had set his jaw. He didn't even intend to lower himself to a response. "We're just goin' for a bite at the cafe," I replied for him. "Why don't you fellas lay off it today, all right?"

Si turned belligerent eyes on me. "Just don't you worry, buster. I was talkin' to the Injun." He immediately turned back to Bill. "What do you need with a cafe, Billy? You got all the free beef you could want over at our place. Gets mighty dark there at night. 'Course you already know that."

Bill's rock-steady gaze met Si's. "We been all through this, Murphy. You got yer cow back, an' she didn't have my brand on 'er, did she? Step out of the way and let us by."

"Yeah, sure. Pretty easy to shrug off, ain't it?" Dick said

belligerently. "You're the one cut that cow outta the herd just hopin' we wouldn't notice."

"Come on, Dick," I retorted. "The sheriff settled all this last spring. Everyone knows Bill ain't no thief. It's others around here we oughtta be worried about."

Si turned on me challengingly. "Meanin' what?"

I sighed. "Just let us by. I've had enough of you for one day."

"Si!"

We all whirled at the sound of Sheriff Rawlings's voice, all except Indian Bill. He continued to stare from Si to Dick, his knees slightly bent as if ready to spring.

Sheriff Rawlings, in spite of his wintry-white hair and gnarled-oak countenance, was a tough man. We all knew it, and he seldom had trouble with the ranching population of that country. He'd never killed a man during his tenure as sheriff, that I knew of, but he'd sure put some egg-sized lumps on a few heads.

"You boys get off the walkway and let 'em pass." The sheriff had a no-nonsense way of speaking, his gruff voice full of the authority of years. "I've had about a belly full of you two."

Si glared at Sheriff Rawlings, but suddenly he turned on his heel and stepped out onto the street, stalking away toward two horses tied in front of the Ranchers Saloon. Dick followed shortly, lengthening his strides to catch up.

Rawlings turned back to me and Bill, smiling. "Couple of idjits." He spat into the dusty street. "Well, how are you two boys, anyway?" He gripped both our hands. "Gettin' ready for the big roundup?"

I nodded. "It's about that time again. Summer sure flew by."

Rawlings met Bill's eyes. "You taggin' along with Tom again?"

Bill smiled. "Sure. He needs all the help he can get." He cuffed me playfully on the shoulder.

"Now don't let 'im get you in any more trouble." He chuckled, winking sideways at me." "An' steer clear of them Murphy boys. They're pure poison."

Bill smiled again. "They're all talk, Sheriff. If it wasn't for you, I reckon I'd just finally take them off behind the barn an' teach 'em some manners."

The sheriff studied Bill a moment with a twinkle in his eye, then looked at me and winked. "You know, I bet he could do it, too. Prob'ly both at once. But seriously, Bill." He met his eyes again. "Just watch out. Si's lookin' for any excuse he c'n find to use that Black-eyed Susan of his. He thinks he's a bad man with a gun. And don't forget something else—whether it's right or wrong, if you win a fight with Si and Dick, they are still white men, and you're still an Indian. Birds of a feather really do stick together when the going gets ugly, and a jury trial could go awful hard on you."

The fall roundup seemed to go by faster than any before it. Bill and I avoided the Murphy boys, and we had no trouble with them. We had a good bunch of cowboys, generally, and in spite of some of them being jealous of Bill, they all got along with him all right. He could sure tell up a story when he became inclined, and many was the night around a roaring cowboy campfire he kept us laughing one minute and on the edge of our bedrolls the next. A time or two he even brought a tear to some hardened eyes. I always admired his way of speaking. Seemed he could put you right where he wanted you and draw you in.

Before we knew it, roundup was over, and although we enjoyed the camaraderie and reckless cow chousing, we were glad it was through, for the growl of an early winter loomed in the air. Of a morning, the clouds across the valley hung low and black, threatening snow. They stayed that way pretty much all day, too, and I spent a lot of time hauling firewood out of the hills, sawing it in lengths and splitting it, getting set for a rough winter. Ice began to clog the creeks, too, and the horses and cattle were growing their coats out extra long.

But one day the sun broke early over the hill, and though there was a promise of winter upon the valley it lifted my spirits.

Sunlight shone gold-yellow off the last of the aspen leaves, and a cold breeze made them sparkle like strings of gold coins.

I guess the weather got to Bill, too, because he rode up to my place in his shirt sleeves with a rifle in his scabbard. "How about going up the valley one last time with me before snow flies, Tom?" he invited. "I spotted a herd of elk that've been feeding late. Some winter meat for both of us."

After two weeks of cutting wood, I didn't hesitate. But I chose to wear a coat, and I ribbed Bill about deciding not to. I reckon I wasn't near as hot-blooded as Bill.

Bill rubbed his hands together briskly. "That's okay," he replied, grinning. "I left my coat laying on the woodpile. I feel like taking a chance today. The cold gets my heart going."

"I thought you were smarter." I laughed and went about gathering my Winchester and a box of shells, then walked out to the corral to catch a horse. I only had two at the place that day, and the one I normally rode had been limping around the day before. So I chose the other one, a knot-headed bay I had to keep a close eye on all the time to keep him from getting in trouble.

When I climbed in the saddle, that bay went to chinning the moon. After he got worn out on that and hadn't dumped me yet, he crow-hopped across the corral, then tried half-heartedly to lay some rail fence—that's cowboy lingo for bucking first one way, then the other, in the shape of a rail fence. For a buster, it was fairly easy riding, after he lost the notion to see over the top of the cabin. I had fun trying to stay on top of a bucking bronc, like most cowboys—us young ones, anyway. That's the only reason I never tried to break the bay of his bad habit. I'm sure Bill could have cured him, if I'd been inclined to let him. Not a one of *his* bucked. Maybe what I didn't know was he was eating the ones that did.

Bill was laughing when I steered the bay back across to the open gate of the round corral. "Better let me take that one for a week or two, Tom. Someday he'll throw you up in the hills an' you'll be walking back home. Or something worse."

I just chuckled. "Heck, pard, I don't wanna take the fun out of the ride! Why don't you stick to freezing to death, I'll stick to riskin' a broke leg. We both choose our poison."

We rode up the canyon, where the sunlight hadn't yet found its way. Mostly we were quiet, enjoying the ride and the pleasant company. The smells of autumn were alluring, and again and again we filled our nostrils. It wasn't singly the aspen, the pine, fir, buck brush, or dead grass. It was all of them. All of them mixed generously into the cold, perfectly clear air of fall.

The horses picked their way through the narrows, the split-rock walls of gray granite rearing up on both sides of us. The creek chuckled along the rock base at our right side, singing us a cheerful song before it would bed down under a coat of ice to await the spring.

At last, we neared Bill's elk feeding ground. To our disappointment, the bright sunlight sparkled in the frosty grass of an empty meadow crisscrossed with fresh elk tracks and droppings.

"Too clear last night," Bill guessed. "They were able to feed all night."

I agreed. "I was afraid of that. We could always get off the horses and hunt the trees. I'm sure they're bedded close by."

Bill hadn't heard me. He was studying something in the grass. I rode closer and saw there was a muddy spot before him where no grass grew. In the center of it was the fresh track of a horse.

I glanced up at Bill. "What do you suppose? Somebody beat us up here and spooked the elk all off?"

Bill shrugged. "Could be. He was here this morning, all right. Let's follow along for a ways. See if he got something."

I was game. I was out for the ride anyway, not so much to bring home an elk. I've always said the work only begins when you put one on the ground, and I didn't savor the idea of me having to walk home while some filthy elk was riding on my horse.

I followed Bill along through the grass, then into the timber. The yellow, frosted grass was pushed down and broken up, and it left a line that might as well have been painted for us. The trail led eventually up out of the trees to a bare, wind-swept ridge.

Up ahead, we heard a horse neigh from a stand of stunted, rustling aspens. Bill and I looked over at each other at the same time. "Wonder if he got somethin'," I said.

"Let's go see."

We started our horses forward, Bill behind me this time. Suddenly, the bay balked at something and began to sidle. I couldn't see what was spooking him, but not being able to bring him in check angered me. I gouged him with the spurs and tried to rein him back onto the path, and he broke into a buck. Only this time he meant it. He lunged and spun, then wheeled the other way, swapping ends. That time he unseated me—me, a self-proclaimed bronc peeler. Down I went, and I landed wrong on my left foot and felt something tear inside. I continued down, sprawling on my side in a pile of rocks.

I could hear the clatter of the bay's hooves as he raced back down the hill. I was hoping Bill would chase him down, but instead he leaped off his horse and ran to my side.

"Hey, pard! You all right?"

My head was spinning, but my eyes focused on his concerned face. "I reckon so, except my left ankle."

When I went to sit up, I quickly found a searing pain in my left ribs, too.

"Just sit there, Tom," Bill ordered. "Breathe easy a while. I'll go catch your horse after a bit, but then we better trade off. You ain't in no shape to ride that knothead."

I chuckled without humor. "Ah, heck. I'm a twister, Bill. I've been stove up worse'n this. You just catch 'im—I'll do the ridin'."

That time Bill just nodded, preoccupied. His horse was shifting around where he had left it ground-reined. It was too well trained to run away, but it sure didn't like something in the wind. Bill cast me a cautious glance, then stood up, making slow tracks in the direction we had been riding. I heard a surprised exclamation.

I tried to turn around to see what Bill was looking at, but it hurt my ribs too badly. I turned back in the other direction and called over to him, "What's wrong, Bill?"

There was only silence.

"Bill, dang it, what'd you find?"

Again silence until I heard him approaching. He came to a stop in front of me and crouched down on his heels. He looked me square in the eyes, glanced off behind me, then returned his eyes to me. "We got trouble, Tom." His voice was quiet, and there was a pallor to his face I'd never seen. "You know Ben Sharp, the school teacher's boy? He's over yonder. Dead."

I stared at Bill in shock, letting his words register on my brain. At last, my lips moved. "Dead? What are you talkin' about?"

Bill just looked over there again. I insisted he help me up, and I leaned on his shoulder to limp over to a pile of jumbled, hat-sized rocks. Ben Sharp lay on his back, staring up at the sky. There was coagulated blood down the side of his head, stiff in his hair. I turned away, half sick. Ben Sharp had been a nice young man. The worst part of it was, he had just married several months ago. He homesteaded a place on the other side of the hill from mine and brought his new wife, Mary, there to live. She was a few months along with child. As of this morning, she was pregnant and a widow.

I gave Bill a grave look, unable to believe what we had stumbled upon. He just smiled sadly. "Well, at least we can take him down to town an' bury him decent. If we hadn't followed him up here, nobody might've found 'im till spring."

He glanced at the sky, and my eyes followed his. In the north, a great black mass of clouds was beginning to pool, and under its belly hung some nasty fingers that seemed to be pointing our way. Bill glanced down at his shirt, over which I had just chided him before leaving my cabin. "North wind's on the move. An' me supposed to be a woodsman, too. Sure hope that coat of mine keeps the woodpile warm."

He looked off in the direction my horse had run. "I'd better go try to round up yer horse, Tom, an' then you c'n ride mine into town. Like it or not, I ain't lettin' you ride a bucker in the shape yer in. So don't even think about arguing. I gotta get goin' 'fore that storm gets any closer. It's gonna be a bad one."

Indian Bill rode off, and I sat alone with the body of Ben Sharp, contemplating the suddenness, the unfairness of death, to take a man so young and with a family building. It just didn't seem right. He had been a nice young fellow. And two mean-tempered brothers like the Murphys still kept walking the earth, making the lives of other people miserable just by their presence.

Nervously, I watched the storm draw nearer, and a stiff wind began to buffet the hill so I had to jam my hands deep in my coat pockets and lower my chin into the sheepskin collar. My backside numbed against my granite slab chair, but I couldn't move around, so I just sat there and prayed my bay hadn't run all the way back to the ranch. I hoped Bill would get back soon.

When I did see Bill coming up the ridge forty-five minutes later, it was just him atop his horse. No bay in sight. By now the wind was bitter cold, and my cheeks and ears had little feeling. I tied my bandana over the brim of my hat, pinning it down over my ears as I watched Bill come up the hill. He stopped in front of me and climbed down stiffly. I noticed his nose, cheeks, and chin were purple.

"Sure is lonesome without my coat," he said, trying to act like he was making a joke. "Well, I couldn't find that nag of yours. He just kept on running. Never did stop, dang knothead. I'm gonna have to just load Ben on his horse an' let you ride mine, an' I guess I'll be doing my own hoofing."

I glanced quickly over at Ben Sharp's body, then back at Bill. "I won't let you do that, Bill. We c'n come back for him with some help. Go fetch his horse, an' I'll ride it. We c'n just drag him into the trees for now. It's not worth you freezin' over. We didn't kill him."

Bill considered this a moment, then nodded. "Yeah, I guess yer right. We c'n come back after the storm blows through."

He trotted off down the ridge into the stand of twisted aspens, and in a few minutes he came back out leading a big buckskin cowhorse, a nice-looking animal but kind of fidgety. "Had his reins caught," Bill said as he led him up to me. "I'll tell you what, Tom. You ride my horse, I'll ride him. He's skittish, an' I ain't gonna trust him with you hurt the way you are. I know mine won't do nothing to hurt you. He's rock-solid if any horse is."

I didn't even try to argue. It was too cold. I looked up at the sky, and the clouds were closing out the blue overhead. A few flakes of snow spat down, but then it quit for a moment. I looked at Bill straightening the buckskin's saddle. He was shivering. I looked over at the warm-looking sheepskin-lined coat Ben Sharp wore.

"Bill, you gotta take his coat off an' wear it. Looks like it'd fit pretty good. Yer gonna freeze to death."

Bill looked at me like he hadn't quite understood what I said. We stared at each other, and then he glanced over at Ben. I guess he knew I was right, for he didn't say a word, just walked over to Ben, and stooping down, worked the coat off Ben's stiff arms. He shrugged into it, and already I could tell he felt better. He looked over at me with a warm look as if thanking me for thinking of him, and then he leaned over and took Ben under the arms, dragging him back down the ridge into the aspens.

Indian Bill helped me climb up on his horse. Then he swung onto the buckskin, and though it pranced nervously it made no move to buck. We started down the ridge with the wind slapping at us. I hugged an arm to my ribs to ease the pain and sank low in my coat.

We had dropped back down the hill to the trail when I heard Bill speak my name from behind. When I turned to look, he was pointing down into the creek bottom. I followed the line made by his finger to a lone, bald-faced black cow that stood down there, back hunched against the wind.

"Can't tell whose it is," I said. "I bet it'll find its way back home tomorrow."

Bill shook his head. "Not the way this storm's shaping up. This trail could be completely snowed in by morning. Reckon we oughtta haze it in with us."

Without another word, Bill reined the buckskin off the trail and down along the creek. As he neared the cow, he stopped suddenly, and I saw him staring at its side where the brand would be. At last, he sort of shrugged to himself and began to turn her. The black cow moved away warily, but with the blizzard blowing in she wasn't in any mood to fight. When he pushed her toward the trail, she went willingly.

The cow passed me as she came onto the trail, and I stared in surprise at the double overbit earmarkings and the brand on her hip. It was the Running M brand. A Murphy cow. I looked up quickly at Bill, who had stopped beside me, and our eyes met and held.

"You actually gonna take that thing in to 'em? You know dang good an' well they wouldn't do it for you."

Indian Bill shrugged. "Who knows. They're cowboys, ain't they? Besides, I ain't doing it for them, I'm doing it for the cow. I don't think she'd last out here once this place snows in."

I watched Bill and shook my head. He was right, of course. It was the code of the range. You found a lost cow, you brought it in. No questions asked. It didn't matter whose cow it was. And Bill had put it right into perspective. It wasn't necessarily for the owners. It was for the cow. We both hated to think of her starving and freezing to death up that canyon. She might just as easily have been one of our own, and those of us who, erroneously or not, considered ourselves the intelligent species had to help out the dumb brutes we passed along our way.

We moved along the trail once more, and now and then a flurry of snow pelted down, convincing us it was the beginning of the big one. But each flurry sort of died before it could really turn into anything serious, and those big black pirate ships of cloud humped together up there above us, glowering and threatening.

Indian Bill rode in the lead now, so he could keep the black cow moving the right direction. She stuck pretty well to the trail now that she was on it. She realized she was headed home, and even though we were facing into the wind she knew shelter and feed lay ahead. That was worth some angry wind in the eyes for a while.

Then at last the snow came down, and for the next three miles it fell like there was no end to it. But down here in the canyon there was only one path to follow, and we stuck to it in the dim light without faltering. Short of going up the steep side of the canyon or down into the creek, there was no way we could take a wrong turn.

I was riding all bent over, nursing my throbbing ribs. I trusted the trail to Bill and just watched the tail of the buckskin, not wanting to look ahead and catch the wind square in my face. Suddenly, Bill's horse came to a stop, and looking up I saw the reason why. Up ahead in the trail sat two riders, hazy in the driving snow. They watched us for a couple of seconds, then rode on to meet us.

As they drew close, I recognized Si and Dick Murphy.

The Murphys drew up, one on either side of the trail. I caught them watching us suspiciously, and as the black cow passed they shot each other a wary glance.

"So." Si Murphy stared at Bill accusingly. "I was right. That's our cow yer pushin' there, Injun. You blind?"

I had ridden up beside Bill now and looked over in time to see the fire begin to build in his eyes. "You couple fools," he said angrily. "Your cow was down in the creek bed fixing t' freeze t' death. I figured I'd bring it in for you."

Si laughed and looked over at Dick, whose confused gaze suddenly disappeared with a laugh of his own. "*You* bring a cow in for *us*? You lyin' Injun!" Si's face had turned suddenly mean. "We both know good an' well you'd never do anything for us. Prob'ly figgered you had some winter meat, eh? Fact is, we missed the old girl this mornin' an' was comin' out t' look for her.

We'd a turned back when the storm hit, but we seen Tom's horse come runnin' on the road an' figgered he was hurt. Now I'm sure glad we didn't turn back."

Indian Bill just watched the Murphys, his eyes full of anger at their stubbornness. I didn't say anything because I was waiting for him to.

"Take yer cow then an' go tell the Sheriff I was stealing it," said Bill evenly. "See if he believes your fool story. Why would I be out in a storm like this trying t' steal a beat up old cow like that?"

Si laughed again. "Great weather t' hide yer crimes, ain't it, Injun?" He spat into the snow that was building up on the trail. "'Sides, why would you be out in weather like this bringin' in somebody else's cows?"

Dick had ridden over closer to us, and I realized he was studying Bill's horse. Suddenly, his eyes widened, and his mouth dropped open. He whipped his head toward his older brother. "Hey, Si. That's Ben Sharp's horse!"

"What the—" Si spurred his horse closer to stare at the buckskin beneath Bill. "Well, sure enough." His eyes narrowed, and I saw his hand move toward the pistol on his hip. "Where's Sharp? *Where is he*?"

Bill sighed. The anger was still in his eyes, but I could see he was starting to grow wary. He had seen Si's hand moving toward his belt gun, and neither of us had any weapon but Bill's Winchester, deep in its scabbard beneath my leg.

"Don't start jumpin' fences you ain't measured," I said suddenly. "We found Ben dead up on the hill. Looked like he got bucked off while he was followin' a herd of elk. Bear musta spooked the horse or somethin'. He was dead an' cold before we ever found 'im."

Si's and Dick's faces turned white, even through the snow, and they stared at each other in shock. They looked back at us, and Si spoke. "How's come you didn't bring Ben out, then? An' what're you doin' wearin' his coat?" he challenged Indian Bill.

Before we knew it he had pulled his pistol and pointed it at us. Dick looked over at him, alarmed, then looked quickly back at us. Following his brother's example, he drew a Smith and Wesson revolver from its holster and cocked it, leveling it on Bill. His eyes were wide and scared, and his mouth hung open. He kept looking back and forth nervously from us to his brother. I was afraid that pistol would go off.

"What're we gonna do, Si? Take 'em in?" By the sick look in Dick's eyes, I think he was afraid of the answer.

"Yeah, we got to," replied Si, but he didn't look at any of us as he said it. "You get down and tie the Injun up, Kincaid," he ordered me, gesturing with his pistol.

I hesitated, and Bill broke in. "His ankle's broke, an' so're his ribs. Horse threw 'im. He can't get down."

"Shut up!" Si spat, staring hatefully at Bill. "All right, you go tie 'im, Dick. Tie 'em both. I'll cover you."

Dick climbed down and did as Si ordered, tying our hands too tightly behind our backs. He was making certain we didn't break free, and my hands started to ache instantly.

When Dick had crawled back into his saddle, Si said, "Now you ride ahead an' keep that cow movin'. I'll stay back here an' watch these two."

We moved along this way for a while, and suddenly I noticed the storm had died down, and there were clear spots of light bluish green sky along the horizon. I sighed with relief for that.

We had gone only about a mile when I heard Si's voice call out behind me. "Dick, hold up."

The younger man stopped and turned his horse, looking past me to see his brother. "What now?" he queried.

"You watch these two. We're all goin' up this here hill."

The hill he had pointed out was a wind-swept, grassy slope speckled with granite boulders. Jagged rocks lined the skyline. And there, toward the top, was one gnarled Douglas fir tree with a long, bare branch that curved and twisted away from the rest of the tree. A cold feeling, colder than my skin, gripped my innards. I studied Si's face, then turned to look at Bill. He only stared up at the tree, his jaw set. He didn't even glance over at me.

"Murphy, what're you up to?" I queried, trying to sound calm. "Trail's straight ahead."

"Just shut up!" Si barked. His eyes stared at me wildly, and with his lower teeth he vigorously chewed the drooping ends of his mustache. It was obvious he had worked himself up to something he didn't want anyone talking him out of.

Si turned to Dick. "I changed my mind, Dick. *I'll* watch these two. You just lead us up toward that lone tree there. Now go on," he urged emphatically, cutting off any forthcoming protest.

Dick's eyes were wide now, his face pale. He looked from us to his brother. But he put spurs to his horse, leaving the black cow where it stood, and started up the steep incline. Both Bill and I just sat our saddles, unmoving, but when we heard Si cock his pistol Bill automatically prodded the buckskin up the hill, letting it follow Dick's horse.

I followed the other two, hearing Si come behind, and our horses slipped and slid in the snowy grass and rocks until we reached the tree. I guess I knew Bill and I were both about to die up here. That bare limb poking out of the other needle-covered branches of the fir told us all we needed to know.

We came to a halt at the big fir, and Si started untying the lasso from his saddle horn. Indian Bill watched him quietly, his face emotionless. "You're making a big mistake, Murphy," he said at last. His voice was a lot calmer than mine would have been. "Everything I told you is true. When you find Ben Sharp, you'll see. He ain't shot or anything. His horse threw 'im off. And fool that I am, I really was bringing that cow in t' be nice. I just didn't want her starving t' death out here. I wasn't bringing her in as a favor t' you, but it would have amounted to the same."

"Yeah, yer a sly one, Injun. Our daddy always told us the only way an Injun c'n live is by stealin', an' I reckon he was right. An' yer all a bunch o' good liars, too. But I ain't buyin' it. I ain't lettin' you go an' have you two leave the country with Ben lyin' up there somewheres with a bullet in 'im. I ain't no fool, no sir!"

Without warning, he flung a loop, and it settled around Indian Bill's neck. Bill took a deep breath and swallowed, and he looked into my eyes. He nodded, almost imperceptibly, and I nodded back, swallowing a big lump in my throat.

Si started his horse toward the tree, jerking the rope tight around Bill's neck so he had to follow. He threw the loose end of the rope over the tree limb, then caught it and tied it securely around his saddle horn.

I stared helplessly at Si. "You two can't be so stupid you think this country will let you get away with killin' two men in cold blood. This is murder. You'll hang, too, if you do this."

"Yeah, sure I will!" Si stared at me, eyes narrowed, fingers turning white as he gripped the saddle horn. "It ain't against the law t' hang a horse thief. Not t' mention a murderer."

I knew Bill was a religious man. He always had been, more so than I. But it was plain he had given up talking to the Murphys, so I spoke up for him. "At least let him say his prayers to his Maker." My voice broke at the end. "Give 'im that, anyhow."

"The hell," growled Si, and with that he kicked the buckskin horse hard in the rump, backing his own horse up to keep the lasso tight.

I stared in horror as Bill's body swung free of the buckskin. My eyes blurred, and I cried out. I begged for them to cut my friend down, but Si only laughed, a wild, crazy laugh. A laugh like he was getting away with some dirty joke at school. Dick sat staring, dumbfounded, and I knew he was sick with fear.

After a minute, Bill had stopped struggling, and I turned to look at Si. His eyes met mine, and we stared at each other for several seconds. It was Si who finally swung his eyes away.

"I reckon you prob'ly wasn't in on killin' Ben Sharp, Kincaid," he said, his voice eerily quiet, monotone.

I continued to stare at him. "Neither was he!" My voice broke again. I swung my eyes from Si to Dick and back, and then to my lifeless friend. "You better kill me, too, Murphy. You better kill me, too."

Si laughed, a heavy sound like he had to force it past his tonsils. "I ain't killin' no white man," he said, riding closer to me until our horses were side by side, facing opposite directions. I saw the blur of his hand as he started to strike out with the barrel of his revolver.

When I regained consciousness, I was all alone on the hill, except for my friend, Bill. I looked up at him from where I lay on the ground. There were tears deep inside me, but I guess they were frozen there from the cold. I just stared, watching his body swing against the stiff breeze, lit dimly by a pink light from the sinking sun in the west.

I sat up, realizing my hands had been cut loose. I stood, and in spite of the burning pain in my ankle I stumbled to where Bill hung. I stopped just short of him and gingerly extended my hand. As soon as it touched his leg, it was as if the whole scene became real, and tears filled my eyes and ran freely down my cheeks. I sobbed and held onto my friend until my soul had run dry. Then I took the knife from my pocket, went to the tree trunk, where Si had tied off the rope, and cut Bill down.

Bill fell with a thud because I couldn't get back to him quickly enough to catch him. He landed in the snow and dead yellow grass, and I slumped down beside him and stared off down the canyon.

Did I say I was alone on the hill? Well, not quite. Bill's horse was there, too. Stealing horses was a hanging offense back then, and I guess to the Murphys' twisted way of thinking it just wouldn't be right to take this one. I don't think they really wanted to kill me, anyway, or I would be swinging up there beside Bill by Dick Murphy's rope. Si had said he wouldn't kill a white man, and taking any transportation from me in this weather would surely have killed me.

I'll never be able to tell how I did it, but I'm sure that patient horse of Bill's did more than I did. Anyway, somehow I got Bill on top of it and then me, too, and we started toward town. We got there about midnight, and I went straight to Sheriff Rawlings's house. My urgent knock brought him to the door. Even though half asleep, he saw the blood plastered in my hair.

"Come in, Tom," he ordered, dragging me by the arm, then shutting the door behind me. He turned up the wick on his kerosene lantern and peered at me closely. "What happened to you?"

I looked at him bitterly. "The Murphys hung Bill!"

After the whole tale came out, the sheriff and I carried Bill's stiff body inside and laid him out on the kitchen table. Mrs. Rawlings had come in, wearing her bed robe and slippers, and she stood at one end of the table, her hands to her mouth, her eyes full of terror.

When we had laid Bill down, I guess we jarred him a little, for a white corner of paper I had not previously seen stuck out of Ben Sharp's coat pocket. Sheriff Rawlings reached over and picked it up, unfolding it. He stared at it for a long time, his lips moving silently as they made out words. At last, he lowered it and looked over at me. He held the paper out to me, and I took it from his fingers.

There were five lines scratched on the paper, made by the lead tip of a bullet, it appeared. It read like this: *I'm in a bad way, my sweet Mary. My horse got spooked by a herd of elk and threw me in some rocks. I fear that I soon will be dead. If anyone finds this here message, please take it to my wife, Mary Sharp, so she'll know. And please take my horse and saddle back to her. It's all I have.* The note ended with Ben Sharp's signature, made by a shaky hand.

I looked up at the sheriff and nodded slowly. I wondered if it would have made any difference if any of us had known this note existed at the time of the hanging. Si had seemed so bent on a killing. I wondered then and always will.

Well, it wasn't much of a trial. It was pretty much cut and dried. I was there four weeks later when they hanged Si Murphy at the gallows. And I was there when the prison wagon came and carted Dick off to a sentence of twenty years in the territorial prison. There was justice, but it came a long ways from bringing back Indian Bill. And believe it or not, there were those who hated me for testifying against the Murphys, for they said I had turned on my own kind. And that's why I had to leave the valley.

But now I've come back to visit a friend, and yesterday I rode by Indian Bill's shack on the creek. It's kind of lonely now, with black windows that stare out at the world like caves. The door hangs loose, with its top hinge broken, and a piece of burlap flutters there in the wind. His horses all went at the county auction, for he had no family. Somebody came by some mighty fine riding animals.

And today I sit here alone with the wind in my hair, staring out over the mountains Indian Bill called home. Well, again, I'm not alone. Remember that horse of Indian Bill's, the one I packed him back to town on? That's the red roan I'm riding now. Sheriff Rawlings let me take him a year ago and saw fit to write me out a bill of sale. So there are two who have come back to visit a friend, and with sadness in our hearts we sit and listen to the wind that moans bittersweet over the grave of Indian Bill.

THE FALL OF
SANTA ANNA

On the hottest of days, the coldest of nights, death never grows weary. And even death can find a use for the hour of *siesta*...

A hot whisper of wind swirled dust across the empty street, rippled the dusty-skinned water in the trough in front of El Rio Colorado Cafe—known to Anglos as the Red River. Along the winding thoroughfare of Alamo, Texas, there was neither sound nor movement. The town's citizens had closed their businesses, gone to their homes to wait out the hottest part of the day.

High above, the sun shone like a brass pendulum, baking the street, bleaching the forlorn adobes. The wind died, and now a solitary drop of water from the mouth of the pump was all that disturbed the filthy surface in the trough. The wasps and beetles there had long since ceased to struggle.

Then, in the north, a small black dot became obvious on the edge of the shimmering horizon. It grew taller as the seconds ticked by, materializing in time into a solitary rider, a man with clothes grayed by miles of desert dust.

The rider was a short man but built well, and he held his back straight, his chin thrust forward. He was dark of hair, dark of eye, cheeks browned by days in the sun. The face was a hard, but not a cruel one, and not unpleasant.

His eyes scanned the empty hitching racks, the lonely staring windows of the adobes, all humble and dust-covered and still. The sun had driven him to remove a linen duster, now tied loosely behind the saddle, but a faded yellow scarf was wrapped around his neck, warding off sunshine, dust, and biting flies. He wore a pin-striped gray wool vest with every button fastened over an off-white muslin shirt, and tan wool pants tucked into flat-heeled square-toed boots. A gray hat with a rounded, battered crown snugged down near his ears, its flat, sweat-stained brim shading his wary face. Yet the shade was inadequate, and drops of perspiration dotted his cheeks.

He carried a Smith and Wesson American forty-four on his left hip. Its walnut grips were scarred but polished smooth. What little steel showed above the rim of the holster was almost free of bluing. Under his left leg rode a '73 Winchester carbine, its wooden stock worn like that of the sidearm.

Beneath the man, a rangy sorrel plodded with head down, half-dozing. Its lower lip hung flaccid, and its toes dragged in the dust, raising a cloud with each step. These hooffalls, the jingling of the man's Texas spurs, and the creaking of the Mother Hubbard saddle were the only sounds of the afternoon.

As the sorrel carried him up the street, the rider's eyes bore into every window, every doorway, every alleyway and side-street. Yet to the casual observer this would not be obvious. He had a way of moving his eyes while pivoting his head very little. The casual observer might also miss the slight cock to the man's left elbow and the way his hand hovered near his holster.

The man rode into the plaza and drew up at a water trough in front of the mercantile store. The sorrel drank long and deep, oblivious to the drowned flies and wasps. The man dismounted and worked the pump handle, and when the water gushed out he removed his hat and bent to let the cool water splash over his head and neck. He took several long, appreciative swallows and straightened to look around him at the quiet town.

Alamo, Texas, in 1885 boasted a population of two or three hundred people, which varied greatly from year to year. A cattle town, they said, inhabited mostly by Mexican ranchers and vaqueros, a few dirt-poor farmers and businessmen, and the occasional drifting prospector. It consisted of the winding, nameless main street and numerous houses, shacks, and businesses scattered with no order across the cactus and grass-dotted plain. The only part of the town laid out with any planning was the plaza. It sat in the center of town, surrounded by the businesses claiming lifeblood status for Alamo, such as El Rio Colorado Cafe, El Lobo Bravo Cantina, La Piñata. Poetic names for run-down buildings more appropriately left unchristened at all. The more reputable businesses such as the mercantile and the barbershop shared the plaza alongside the cantinas and lower class establishments, for this was the hub of the town's activity, and those with any capital had picked this prime location.

On one end of the plaza was a brush *jacale* offering shade and several wicker chairs for the rest of weary travelers. The stranger had picked up the sorrel's reins and started toward that sanctuary when he saw his first living being since entering the town.

The man was a Mexican, slightly shorter than the gringo, plump in build with stunted fingers and prying eyes. He peered at the stranger from the doorway of El Lobo Bravo. His shirt was wrinkled and sweat-stained, buttoned at sleeve and collar, and suspenders held up dirty tan pants.

Their eyes met for several seconds, and neither man smiled. When the stranger started across the fifty feet of wheel-rutted street between them, the Mexican turned back inside the establishment.

The man stopped at the sagging hitching rail in front of El Lobo Bravo and glanced one more time about the town. Another breeze whipped dust off the mud roof of the cantina, pelting his cheeks with tiny particles. He wiped wearily with his sleeve at the sweat on his face, then untied the sorrel's lead rope from the saddle horn and swung it around the rail. Tired as the animal was, even if it worked the rope loose it would not go far.

Inside the cool shadows of the cantina, the stranger let his vision adjust to the dim light. The man he had seen outside stood behind a battered plank bar, watching him through noncommittal eyes. The stranger's gaze perused every corner of the room, the unoccupied tables and rickety chairs, the whisky-stained dirt floor, a poor-quality painting of a gaudily-dressed *señorita* dancing in a room full of men with blank, staring faces. Seeing the room was empty of patrons, he moved to the bartender and faced him across the narrow bar.

"Mescal," he ordered. "And water it down by half."

The Mexican looked at him furtively but didn't meet his eyes. He dipped his head in an almost imperceptible nod, reached under the bar, and drew forth a dark brown, half-empty bottle. Deftly, he poured two fingers' *mescal* into a glass, then filled the rest with water.

"You are new in Alamo. Jus' trav'leen through?"

The newcomer squinted up from his drink, then nodded. "I've some business here, then I'll be movin' on." He swished the mixture around in his glass, looked down at it and frowned, then took a swallow, wincing as it went down.

The Mexican gazed past the stranger out into the sunlit street, then looked back at him.

"You workeen? What do you do?"

The stranger scratched his whiskered jaw, looking down the long bar rather than into the Mexican's curious eyes. "I've heard there's a man I need to see that lives here in Alamo. Just need to deliver him a message."

The Mexican nodded. "Who is he? Could be I know heem."

This time the man looked over, and their eyes met. "Name's Rudd Cale. Great big fella, yellow hair."

The bartender narrowed his eyes, turned his head slightly sideways. He peered at the stranger for several seconds. Finally, he lifted his head in acknowledgment. "*Si.* I know *Señor* Cale. Everyone know *Señor* Cale."

"Know where I might find him?"

The Mexican shook his head without pause. "He is a beezy man, *Señor* Cale. Could be anywhere. Wha's your name? Why you look for heem? Maybe I tell heem."

"Name's Boon."

"Boon, ay? Well, wha' do you weesh I shou' tell heem? If I see heem, of course. Could be he weel stop here today. You never know."

Boon shrugged. "I can't really say. It's a personal matter, sort of. Just tell 'im Boon's lookin' for him. Nothin' more."

The Mexican continued to eye Boon. "It's a friendly matter, I hope, that you weesh to speak of. If not, it could go bad for a leetle man like you."

Boon's face went hard, but he just nodded. Not an argumentative man, he saw no need to bring up the fact that he was taller than the bartender. He downed the rest of his drink in several swallows and winced, and when his throat stopped burning he wiped his mouth and looked back up at the Mexican.

"Well, you see Mr. Cale, you just tell 'im a man by name of Boon wants to see him. *Gracias.*"

Boon pushed a silver coin and his empty glass toward the Mexican with the tips of his fingers, turned and strode to the door. He stood in the doorway for a moment, eyeing the town. Standing with the Mexican at his back was uncomfortable, so he didn't pause long. He walked to the hitching rail and picked up the sorrel's lead rope. The dozing horse lifted its head slightly and blew through its nostrils, rolling its eyes.

Kitty corner across the plaza, El Rio Colorado Cafe sported two uncharacteristically large windows, one on each side of its royal blue plank door. Boon caught movement from the corner of his eye and looked toward the cafe in time to see someone slide curtains to either side of the left window. They followed the same procedure at the second window, and still Boon made out the form of the person only vaguely but guessed it to be a woman from what little he could make out through the filmy glass.

Then, as he stood in the center of the plaza watching, the big door creaked open, and she stepped into the sunlight.

The woman's hair was shiny and black, tied in a queue and

hanging behind her back. She wore a white blouse and red skirt with a snug waist that accentuated her figure. She moved gracefully and slow enough so Boon assumed she had seen him and knew his eyes were on her.

Forgetting the wicker chairs in the shade, Boon turned toward the cafe. His walk was soft-footed, smooth. He stopped in front of the cafe, and the woman stood watching as he tied his lead rope to one of the two rails there.

Up close, this woman was very pretty, with dark eyes pleasantly mischievous in their steady gaze, her cheeks aglow with a slight blush. Her lips were parted to reveal white teeth, and a smooth and slender neck swept down into the top of her blouse. The woman obviously carried Mexican blood, but she had Caucasian in her ancestry, also. Her eyes studied Boon, and when their gazes met, they held for several seconds. It was he who broke the silence.

"Hello. You opening for business?"

Though her face was pleasant, her eyes touched with favorable appraisal, the woman did not smile. She just nodded and pushed the door open a little wider.

"Go ahead and come inside," she said in a good American accent.

The woman turned and entered the cool shadows of the establishment, and Boon followed, happy to be out of the sun again and drawn by the smell of frying meat. As he walked, he tried to beat some of the dust from his clothes with his hat. He sat at a table against the far wall and set his hat on the chair beside him. His dark hair fell across his forehead, and he swept it back with his hand.

The woman came to him with a tin pitcher. "The water is cool," she stated. "Or also there is *cerveza, tequila,* and *mescal.* Are you a drinking man?"

Boon found a slight smile tugging at the corner of his mouth. This woman seemed to have decided the answer before even coming to his table.

"I'll take the water, ma'am. You already have it, and I have a powerful thirst that alcohol would only make worse."

She poured a glass full of water and set it before him. "You have a big appetite, I think," she said frankly, looking him over. "A plate of *frijoles*, *tortillas*, and beef is fifty cents. There is also an apple pie, if you like sweet food."

"Thanks for the suggestion. I reckon I'll take the *frijoles* and *tortillas*, but do you have chicken instead of the beef?"

She shook her head. "No, only beef. The icehouse was emptied early this year. What we kill must be eaten as quickly as possible."

"All right, beef it is then. What else is there in Texas, anyway?"

"And the pie?"

Boon glanced about the empty room before he answered, then returned his eyes to hers. "I'll take the pie on one condition."

The woman paused, then raised a brow. "And that is?"

"You'll sit and have a piece of it with me. I'll buy yours, too."

This time she laughed, and though Boon did not consider himself a romantic man he was moved by the light in her eyes and the way the laugh wrinkles cut in to surround them. He continued to look at her frankly, not hiding his admiration of her looks.

"Do you care if I am married?" she asked bluntly.

For no reason he could understand, something inside Boon fell, but he did not let on. He chuckled and thought for a moment. "I only want to talk, ma'am," he replied. "So no, I don't care. But you aren't married anyway," he added on a whim.

A surprised look crossed the woman's face, and for a moment she was silent.

"You are very sure. How can you say that?"

"I say what comes to mind, and it comes to my mind that you don't look married."

She nodded, then smiled, obviously a little embarrassed. "You are right, this time. But I was. My husband died one year ago. All right. I will sit with you, as long you're the only one here. It has been quiet today."

Before Boon could even think to offer condolences, the woman walked away and disappeared behind a partition where a thin veil of smoke seeped out. When she returned, she carried two plates and a tin of apple pie. She set one plate before Boon and served him a large piece of pie, and he looked at it curiously, then up at her.

"Dessert before dinner?"

"Why not? Maybe I thought you could use a little sweetening up," she said with a mischievous smile.

She served herself, then sat down directly across from Boon and picked up a fork, and when she looked back up their eyes met. He read her curiosity. She stared at him for several seconds, a half-bemused look about her eyes and mouth, almost like she was about to smile again but was holding it back.

She dropped her eyes and waved her fork in front of her. "This American food is not bad. Not like Mexican food, but not bad."

Boon took a bite of his pie, and its tart sweetness made his cheeks almost pucker. "Very good. My compliments."

The woman shrugged. "I didn't make it. Pedro is the cook."

"Well, pass it on to Pedro, then. He makes a pretty good pie, for a Mexican." He paused for a moment. "You have some American in you, if my guess is right."

"*Sí*. My father's father was white. My mother's father was Mexican. They died together at the Alamo."

"My grandfather died there, too," replied Boon.

While gazing past Boon at the wall, the woman took a bite of her pie and chewed silently for a moment before swallowing. Then she looked back at him and her lips parted like she was about to speak.

"They call me Boon."

She blinked with surprise and stared at him for a moment. Suddenly she laughed, her eyes twinkling.

Boon smiled. "What's funny about that?"

"Oh, nothing. I'm sorry. You just… Well, you read my mind. I wanted to ask your name, but they tell me that's impolite."

"Impolite, huh? Well, what's *your* name?"

She looked at him boldly. "So it is *you* who are impolite. All right. My name is Carmen. Carmen Esperanza."

"Good to meet you, Mrs. Esperanza," said Boon with a nod. "And I don't mean to be impolite, but sometimes I'm in a hurry. A man can't wait forever for someone to offer some things."

"Oh, I was only making a joke. Please don't be offended. And please call me Carmen." She took another bite of pie and chewed deliberately while avoiding his gaze. Then she looked back. "So why are you in such a hurry?"

Boon swallowed. "Well, Carmen, I don't figure to be in town long. I came here lookin' for a man. An old acquaintance of mine."

"Who is that?"

"He used to go by the name of Rudd Cale. Do you know him?"

Carmen's face went serious at that name, and she stopped chewing and searched Boon's eyes for several seconds with questions bouncing behind hers. He met her gaze.

"Yes, I know Señor Cale. He owns this building and half the others in town. In fact, I guess you could say he owns the town itself."

Boon could not hide the surprise in his eyes as he sank back in his chair and stared past the woman toward the counter. The revelation explained something he had always wondered about. Cale had come by a large sum of money fifteen years ago, and Boon always assumed he would blow it on women and whisky. Maybe the man was smarter than he had given him credit for.

Carmen gathered his mood and was quiet, watching him with curious eyes. Finally, she broke the uncomfortable silence. "How do you know Señor Cale? What do you wish with him? Is he a friend?"

Boon looked over at her and straightened back up in his

chair. He watched her for a moment, trying to read what she was thinking. What did Cale mean to her, if anything? Was he only an employer, or something more?

"You couldn't call us friends, ma'am. Just old acquaintances. But I carry some information he'd be powerful interested to know. Concerns some mutual friends of ours."

"If you are not friends, I hope at least you are not enemies," said Carmen. "Señor Cale is a very powerful man, and he always has many men with him. I hope you bring him news that is good."

Boon shrugged, uncertain just how much he could divulge. It was not as if he knew this woman. She was just a pretty stranger. Carmen stared at him, searching his eyes. Finally, she looked away.

"You are not a peace officer, are you?" She met Boon's eyes again. "I think it might be very bad for you, if you are. There was a marshal here, maybe two years ago. He was looking for Señor Cale, too, and one day he just disappeared. No one ever found him."

Boon nodded slowly, letting that information sink in while he chewed a bite of pie. The land was wild out here. Many unfortunate accidents might befall a man riding the rough country. Anything might have become of the marshal Carmen spoke of. But knowing Rudd Cale's past, Boon would not put anything past him. He would commit very desperate deeds to gain his desires. The chances he was behind the marshal's disappearance were just as good as otherwise.

"No, Carmen, I'm not carrying a badge," replied Boon at last. "Too much responsibility. Just a message. And what about you? With your husband gone, why do you stay in Alamo? It doesn't seem like much of a town for a woman like you."

Carmen laughed. "A woman like me? What kind of a woman is that?"

Boon felt himself blush. "Well, you understand what I— I just mean to say it seems you might have more of a chance to find yourself someone new in a place like Santa Fe, or Denver, or

San Francisco. A city. This place seems like a dead-end to me."

"Many times I have thought of leaving, Señor Boon. I admit the cities do beckon with their wonders. But I am a simple woman, and this is my country. I grew up here. I can't believe the man who would replace my husband lives in a city such as San Francisco. He would be a quiet, strong man, a man of the desert."

"There are men like that everywhere, Carmen—don't be fooled. A city is just a gathering spot, and many good men are passing through to better places. You oughtta go see, just for yourself. You'll be surprised."

Carmen shrugged. "Perhaps I will one day. Alamo is not the village it was when Señor Cale first came here. It lost its innocence, I think. I feel I will not stay here forever. So then if you are not a peace officer, what *do* you do for a living?" she asked abruptly.

There was a lengthy pause as Boon chewed a mouthful and avoided looking at Carmen. He was aware of her eyes on him. His own finally met them.

"I do whatever I can to keep me alive, I reckon. I don't hold down a job long. You see, I've been looking for Cale for a long time. A very long time."

As Boon finished speaking, he heard hooffalls, and outside a horse blew. He looked that way. Two men were riding up to the front of the cafe, two white men, gunmen, by the look of their rigs. They stepped into the street wearily, slapped their hats against their thighs, and walked through the front door.

He turned to look at Carmen, and she was watching the newcomers enter. She turned back toward Boon, and the twinkle in her eyes disappeared. "I'd better not talk anymore, Señor Boon," she whispered. "I have to go."

She stood and was about to turn from the table when Boon snatched her wrist in his strong hand. She looked down at his hand, then up at his eyes, and he caught a look of worry in hers.

"Please."

"But you haven't finished your pie," he said.

"No. I really must go. I really must."

Boon opened his hand, allowing Carmen to retract her arm. She thanked him with her eyes and turned toward the other men.

In silence, Boon chewed his pie and watched with veiled curiosity the interaction between Carmen and the two newcomers. It was obvious these men frequented the place, for they used Carmen's name freely. But even though she seemed to know them, Carmen only referred to them once by name, and then she just used "sir". Her manner of speaking was courteous, but not spontaneous, almost as if she were afraid to say the wrong thing to them or was afraid what they might say to her. She took their orders, then departed as quickly as she could.

For a few more moments, Boon studied the pair discreetly. Who were they? And why did they frighten Carmen so? Were they indeed gunmen, as he suspected? Perhaps part of this entourage Rudd Cale was reported to surround himself with? They were rough-looking and acting men, obviously accustomed to having their way. How would they greet strangers to their town? Considering Rudd Cale's past, it was probable he was suspicious of anyone riding in, especially anyone who looked the part of a gunman, as Boon guessed he did. But did Cale prefer to handle strangers himself or allow his hired men that privilege?

A minute after Carmen left the room, hooves clopping in the thick dust of the street again drew Boon's casual interest. He watched riders, this time three of them, pull up and climb off their horses in front. They sauntered into the cafe, two Mexicans and a white man, and exchanged conversation boisterously with the two men already present, referring to one another by nicknames or through a very casual use of their last names.

The three new ones seated themselves at a table near the counter and turned to look Boon over with open disdain. One of them made a whispered comment to the other two, who laughed out loud, and then one of those two leaned across to the other pair and shared the same joke with them. Boon turned bored eyes from them.

Several minutes passed while Boon wished he were some place away from these newcomers' foul and loud mouths. At last, Carmen came back into the room carrying a tray and walked to his table. Thinly veiled warning was in her eyes when they met Boon's as she leaned down to deposit the tray before him. She flashed her eyes toward the door.

"Hey, Carmen."

At the sound of the voice, the Mexican woman closed her eyes resignedly, but when she opened them again they held a look of renewed urgency for Boon. She turned toward the speaker, the white man who had come in with the Mexicans.

"Yes, Señor Horne?"

Horne was a big man, eight inches taller than Boone, and a new Colt forty-five rode his right hip in plain sight. "Carmen, honey, there's five of us. What the hell you doin' servin' some saddle bum first? We're workin' men, and we're in a hurry."

"Sorry, Señor Horne." Carmen's voice was timid, a tone unbefitting what Boon had seen of her so far. "He came in first."

"Well, what he's havin' looks good to me. Bring his over here an' let me make sure it's not too hot for him." Horne laughed, but it was not a good-natured laugh. He was not joking.

"Yours will be right out, Señor Horne," she replied. Almost as an afterthought, she hurried toward their table. "How would you like some pie while you wait?" She purposely stopped in front of Horne, blocking his view of Boon.

There was a moment's hesitation while the room was deadly still. One of the Mexicans said something to the other in Spanish, and they laughed. Then Horne laughed, too, very loud and harshly.

"Sure, Carmen, bring us all a round of pie. And bring some of that mescal."

As Carmen walked toward the kitchen, she again looked warningly at Boon, then disappeared behind the partition.

Boon ate slowly, deliberately. He had a stubborn streak, and it surfaced now. He knew when he was being pushed, and this man Horne was pushing him, even though he had not spoken one word directly to him. He was familiar with his breed. Even now his mind probably churned while he sought something new to say to vex him. Boon made up his mind right then he would not be the first man to walk out of this room. He would not be cowed, and he would not leave here with these *hombres* thinking they had scared him off.

So he took his bites slowly, setting his fork down after each one and chewing with care. He made a point of not looking at the gunmen, but he could feel their scrutiny.

The men had been talking among themselves, but Boon knew by the change in Horne's tone when the talk was again directed at him.

"Hey, Garcia. Ain't you kinda sweet on ole Carmen, there? If I was you, I'd watch that gent. When we come in, there was two plates at his table. I think he's movin' in on her."

"Ees that so?" Garcia tried to sound mean. "What're we gonna do about it?"

"Well, I say we tie 'im t' that busted down nag outside and chouse 'em both outta town."

"Señor Horne, *please,*" came a new voice from the back of the room.

Boon looked up to see a tall, thin Mexican standing back at the room's partition with Carmen at his side. Boon took this to be the cook, Pedro.

"I don't think Señor Cale would want any trouble in his place, do you?" Pedro asked.

"Well, he ain't here. Besides, this fella ain't got the nerve to cause anyone much trouble. He's kind of a shy one."

Boon had stopped chewing at the sound of Cale's name. Now he turned his head and met Horne's gaze.

"What do you have to do with Rudd Cale?"

Surprise flashed across Horne's face as he looked around at

his cohorts, unsure how to take the question. But Horne quickly composed himself and edged his chair away from the table.

"I work for 'im. Who's askin'?"

"The name's Boon. I'm here to see Cale. He around?"

Horne shrugged. "Well, that depends. What do you want with him?"

"I have a message," said Boon, taking another bite of beef. "A message he probably won't be happy to hear, but he will."

"Well, I'll shore give him the message, mister, an' then you c'n make tracks. I don't think we want you in Alamo."

Boon gazed at Horne for several seconds and then chuckled. "I don't much care what you want. Just give Cale the message that I'll be comin' to see him personally. I won't be leavin' town until we meet."

Horne shoved back his chair and stood up. "Boys, this shore sounds like a challenge to me," he growled. "The little man thinks he's a curly wolf."

Garcia laughed. "Well, go take heem, hombre. Or you need help?"

Horne flashed an angry glance toward the Mexican and started across the floor.

Boon remained seated. He picked his fork up in his right hand, his non-gun hand, and took a mouthful of beans. He watched Horne intently, but his only further movement was that of his jaw as he chewed.

Horne stopped at the edge of Boon's table. "Get up, loud-mouth. When I say we want you gone, you better leave. I don't give no second chances."

Without warning, Horne swung at Boon's face with an open palm. What happened next was so fast most of them in the room could not say for sure what occurred until it was all over. Boon ducked his head, at the same time swinging his right fist around with the fork. Horne's hand just skimmed the top of Boon's head as the fork sank into his cheek clear to the juncture of the tines. Horne let out a scream and staggered back, the fork still protruding from his cheek. There was a second while he just stared at Boon, eyes wide with shock, and then with an oath he went for his gun.

As if by magic, Boon was on his feet, and his Smith and Wesson appeared cocked in his left fist, its bore lined up with Horne's chest. The little man stood there long enough to let the situation sink into Horne's muddled mind. Horne's knuckles had gone white around his still-holstered Colt, and he just stared down the hollow bore of the forty-four, the fork protruding from his cheek. As yet, the wound was blocked by the tines and had not commenced to bleed.

"Now you boys just pay for your meals, leave a tip for Carmen, there, and ease out that front door," said Boon quietly. "I could've killed your friend here, but instead I just gave him somethin' to remember me by. So don't any of you press your luck by waitin' on me outside. I got a Winchester under my saddle that'll kill you just as dead as this pistol. Remember, I didn't ask for this trouble."

"We ain't even ate," said one of the white men who had come into the cafe first, his shocked eyes flickering to the fork that stuck out of his comrade's face. "What do we have to pay for?"

"You pay for Pedro's trouble or Carmen's worry, or maybe just yer rest in the shade of this roof. But pay, whatever you wanna tell yourself it's for. If you don't, we'll finish this right here. And remember what I said. I want you to tell Rudd Cale I'm comin' to see him. An' he just as well be wearin' a gun when I do."

The Alamo Hotel stood on the far edge of town, rearing from the very earth in the middle of the stark desert like some mighty fortress. It was a grand structure, much too rich, it seemed, to be here in the middle of nowhere. Its two stories of white frame construction, surrounded by gray mesquite and prickly pear, towered above the rest of the town, and three steps led up to its long porch, where several loungers sat in chairs and watched Boon ride slowly up. Above the porch was a balcony stretching the full length of the building, and over it in huge red letters were the words, THE ALAMO.

Carefully watching the silent onlookers while seeming to hardly notice them, Boon drew in at the long, carved hitching rail and climbed down. He tied the sorrel to the rail among several other horses and went up the porch with his hand swinging near the butt of his gun.

His heart pounded. His nerves twitched, anticipating. This was Rudd Cale's hangout, Carmen had told him. He owned the Alamo, along with most of the town. With any luck, Cale would be here now, and if so he would meet his maker. After Boon's many years of weary searching, Cale could no longer hide. The big man's time had come to pay for his crimes. His judge *and* jury had arrived. But most importantly his executioner.

Inside, the Alamo's opulence continued to astound the traveler. Boon's eyes swept over the varnished hardwood floor to the red-carpeted, banistered staircase. They took in the long mahogany bar with the finely carved borders and the brass foot rail. Behind the bar hung a wide, spotless mirror, its border decorated with painted red flowers. And above the bar, hanging high on the wall, perched an idealized painting of the mission that had given its name to this town and this hotel. In front of the mission, waving his sword as he wheeled his big black horse, was the Mexican dictator, General Antonio Lopez de Santa Anna.

Boon felt his stomach turn inside him. It sickened him to see another American, especially one who called himself a Texan, seem to pay so much reverence to the man who had dealt Texas its most severe blow. Besides the grandfather Boon had lost at the Alamo, the famed mission of San Antone, he had many friends who had lost relations there. And it was Santa Anna who brought that beloved mission and its heroes to the ground. The part that cut deepest of all was what lay behind the Mexican, the Alamo itself, falling in ruin as smoke rose into the sky in great black clouds.

Behind the bar stood a man with wavy white hair and an

honest looking face. It was apparent from the look he gave Boon, however, that Horne and the others had been here before him.

"You must be the one they call Boon."

"I am."

"Well, I'm Anson Hipe. I run this hotel. And I've been instructed to tell you you'll not be served under this roof."

Boon ignored Hipe's words. "They tell me Rudd Cale owns this place."

"He does," replied Anson Hipe. "That he does. I'm afraid I'm going to have to ask you to leave, Boon," said Hipe suddenly. "Some of Mr. Cale's boys are upstairs, and we don't want any trouble in here."

"When will Cale be in?" asked Boon. "Or will he? You don't think he's afraid of me, do you?"

Hipe chuckled. "I hardly think so, mister. I hear you got lucky enough to get the drop on Joe Horne, but we've all seen Rudd Cale shoot. He'd be a hard one to beat."

"Well, I'll have to kill him or he'll have to kill me," said Boon matter-of-factly. "Otherwise, I'm in town to stay."

"Just what is it you have against Mr. Cale? I want you to know he has given an awful lot of folks around here a fair shake. He always seemed like a pretty fair man, and mighty generous. I'd have been jobless myself, without him."

Boon glanced around at the other men in the room, who all stared at him with open malice. Then he looked back at Hipe.

"You seem to be a fair man, Hipe, and if you really want to know, I'll tell you about Cale. Is there some place we can talk in private?"

Hipe looked around the room hesitantly. Several of the loungers looked at him with warning in their eyes, but that only seemed to help him decide.

"Sure. Come to the back room."

Boon followed Hipe into a tidy little office behind the bar, stark except for a desk, several chairs, and a red, braided rug on the floor. Hipe walked over and seated himself on the edge of the desk, his blue eyes meeting Boon's.

"Say your bit, mister, and then I want you to leave. I'm hearing you out to be fair, but I can't see turning against a man who's helped me out like Cale has."

"Fair enough," replied Boon. "But I might change your mind about our friend Cale. And so you don't think I'm lyin,' take a look at this while I talk."

He reached inside his vest and withdrew a sheet of yellowing, wrinkled newspaper, folded very carefully. He unfolded it and handed it and a wanted poster to Anson Hipe. On the poster was a likeness of Rudd Cale, and the poster, out of Tennessee, offered a reward of five hundred dollars, dead or alive. Hipe's eyebrows raised in surprise, and he turned his attention to the newspaper, which was printed in Memphis. His eyes narrowed as he read, his lips silently forming the words.

Twenty minutes later, the door to Hipe's office creaked open, and first Hipe, then Boon stepped back into the room. Anson Hipe's face was pale, as if he were ill. He walked to his place behind the bar while Boon went back to the other side, and Hipe's eyes were downcast, away from the curious gazes of the other men there.

"What'll you have, Mr. Boon?"

"Be careful, Anson," piped up one of the men seated at a table. "You know how Mr. Cale will take this."

"Doesn't matter, Benson. I'm through here. This is my last day in Alamo," said Hipe, his voice shaky. "I'm through with Rudd Cale. What'll you have, Mr. Boon?" he repeated.

Boon ordered a diluted whisky. It was as much for Hipe as for himself. He knew the old man wished to make a show of going against Cale by serving him, and he did not want to take that satisfaction away from him. With the whisky before him, Boon picked it up and sipped gingerly. He set it back on the bar.

When the swinging doors creaked, everyone turned to them. Boon's eyes lit up, in spite of himself, when he saw Carmen Esperanza walking toward him, her face full of worry. She stopped when close and put her hand on his sleeve.

"I came as soon as I heard, Señor Boon. You must leave here at once. Señor Cale is coming. He is very bad and very fast, and he has many men with him. Please don't stay. I made a mistake telling you where he would be, and I'm sorry. Please don't let this thing be my fault, for speaking of this place to you."

Boon smiled and patted Carmen's hand. "Thanks for your concern, Carmen. But I can't leave now, not without Cale. I might as well be dead myself as walk out of here without him. And don't worry. Sooner or later, someone else would have told me of this place, if only to see what Cale would do when he found me."

Carmen opened her mouth to speak, but her intended pro-test was drowned out by the sound of many horses loping up to the front of the building.

"You'd better leave, Carmen. Please. This won't be somethin' you need to see."

Carmen looked into his eyes, and hers were pleading. She gazed at him, then sighed at last and dropped her hand from his sleeve. "I am sorry for you, Señor Boon. I have to say, there are many men larger than you, but you are the first real man this town has seen since my husband died. But you cannot fight Rudd Cale and live. He has too many with him. *Adios, valiente.*" *Good-bye, brave man...*

Carmen backed away as tears welled up in her eyes.

There was a great commotion on the porch, many boots tromping across it, and the swinging doors flew wide. Rudd Cale made an impressive silhouette, his broad shoulders darkening the doorway. But his outline was overcome by the horde of men who pushed behind him to enter. He came into the room, and his men fanned out around him.

Cale stood at least a head taller than Boon and outweighed him by sixty pounds. The dusty brim of his hat shaded short-clipped blond hair, and a moustache drooped to the edge of a broad, whiskered jaw. On his hip, his Colt Peacemaker was worn and well-used, its ivory grips shimmering softly in the dim lamplight.

Cale's pale blue eyes scanned the room quickly and came to light on Boon. A smirk spread his whiskers, and he walked up to the bar, fifteen feet down from Boon, and leaned his left side against it, resting a hand on its top.

"You must be the little man with the fork. Everybody's talkin' about you, little man. They say you have a message for me."

Boon looked Cale up and down. Then he smiled, but he did not speak. Reaching down, he picked up his glass and took another sip.

Cale's eyes narrowed then widened, and his lips pursed. Suddenly, he laughed, a harsh, booming sound in the silence of the room. He looked over at Hipe. "Give me a brandy, Anson. A big one."

Hipe stared at Cale, his eyes as cold as Boon's. He slid a dark brown bottle across the bar toward Cale, then a glass, but he made no move to pour.

"Pour it, man," growled Cale.

"You'll have to do that yourself," said Hipe. "I don't work here anymore."

The big man looked over at Hipe and stared. "What the hell is this? I said *pour.*"

Hipe looked Cale in the eyes as he peeled off his apron.

"And I said you'll have to pour it yourself."

With a murderous look in his eyes, Cale cursed the old man and plucked the cork out of the bottle, then tilted it and filled the glass to the top. Picking up the glass, Cale put it to his lips, and throwing his massive head back he downed it in several loud gulps. He smiled then, a forced smile to hide the way the alcohol burned.

Cale turned his attention back to Boon, who stood silent.

"I'll ask you again, little man. What's your message?"

Boon leaned against the bar, staring at the glass before him. To all outward appearances he was relaxed, and he took another sip from his whisky glass. But inside he was a mass of ticking nerves, tensed like the hammer of a gun ready to go off. He waited, deliberately holding his silence. He knew Rudd Cale, knew his streak of impatience. Cale hated to be ignored. He became furious. He lost his power of deliberation then, acting on instinct alone. It was this Boon hoped to achieve.

"Well, have you lost your tongue?" Cale boomed. "I don't have all day here."

Boon took another sip of his liquor, looked up at Anson Hipe and gave a wink. But he remained silent.

Cale's face began to redden. He swept the room with his eyes, then returned them to Boon. Scowling, he rubbed his hand across his mouth. Suddenly, his eyes narrowed, and he leaned forward to peer closer at Boon.

"Hey, I know you from somewhere, don't I?"

Boon turned to face him fully, his hand dangling near his holster. He stared at him for a long ten seconds. "I don't know, do you?"

"Damn right. Where from?"

"Think back, Rudd. Way back."

Rudd Cale spat. He reached up and loosened his collar and looked around him at his men again, then at Boon.

"While you're thinkin,' have another drink, Rudd. I'll be here all day."

"No, mister," boomed Cale. "I won't wait no more. You came huntin' me with a message to give. Deliver it and get out of my town. Now."

"All right, Rudd. My name doesn't mean anything to you, huh? How about Phoebe Cale? John Cale? How about those names? Phoebe died, too, Rudd. She died of a broken heart."

This cryptic message drew puzzled glances from the onlookers, but Cale's eyes widened like he was looking at the devil himself. His lip quivered and his hand tensed near his gun.

"You..."

The big man's hand swept down and clutched the Colt.

Prepared for the sudden move, Boon palmed his own forty-four and cocked it as he heard the explosion of Cale's Colt and saw the barrel lunge and erupt with flame and smoke. The bannister behind Boon took Cale's bullet, scattering splinters. Boon heard it, far back in his consciousness, but his instincts drove him now. They drove his hand to rise, almost straight out from his body. They drove his finger to squeeze the trigger, his thumb to bring back the hammer again. Four shots he fired in quick succession, all of them into an area the size of a saucer in Cale's broad chest.

Cale's Colt exploded once more, but the bullet was unguided and struck the nail above the bar where the portrait of Santa Anna and the Alamo hung. Anson Hipe barely dodged the falling frame as it struck the bar and broke into pieces before him, most of them falling to the floor.

Rudd Cale bled profusely, leaning against the bar, eyeing Boon with shocked eyes. He was already dead, and everyone knew it except for him. "You..." He stared gray-faced at Boon. "You're that... little runt my folks... took in. Why, you little..."

Cale's gun hung useless from the tips of his fingers. A shudder ran through his body and his neck convulsed. His knees suddenly gave out, and he flopped to the bloody floor, his gun skittering away across the hardwood.

"Don't even think about it!"

Boon heard Anson Hipe growl the words, and turning he saw the old man with a double-barreled shotgun in his hands, both hammers drawn back. The barrels were levelled at Cale's men, some of whom had started to reach for their guns. "I don't want any more blood shed in here, boys, but if you try and touch this man I'll drop you where you stand."

No one accepted the challenge. The toughs backed toward the door.

Boon felt a touch on his arm and whirled about with his gun in his hand. He came face to face with Carmen Esperanza.

"I couldn't go until I knew... I had to make sure you were all right," she said.

Boon tried to smile. "Thank you, Carmen. I'm fine. Cale always had a way of gettin' real upset when folks didn't respond to him the way he thought they should. It made him careless, and then he couldn't hit a thing with that iron."

"Why did you hate him so much?"

"Let Mr. Hipe tell you, Carmen. It's time I got out of this town while I'm able," he said with a glance at the group of red-faced men.

While Hipe held the shotgun on Cale's men, Boon reloaded his weapon, then backed to the swinging doors.

"Thanks for the hand, Hipe," he said to the bartender, and then he stepped outside.

Carmen followed him onto the porch without asking his permission. "I suppose you have someone waiting for you at home, Señor Boon," she said bluntly. "And I'm not welcome there. If that's so, tell me before I say anything else and make a fool of myself."

"There's nobody, Carmen," Boon replied. "I spent the last fifteen years lookin' for Rudd Cale, and there wasn't time for anyone else. And call me Boon, please. My name's Boon Cale."

Carmen's mouth dropped open. "You were related?"

"His parents adopted me when I was five. Back then I went mostly by my middle name of James, so Rudd didn't remember the name Boon. Well, he decided he didn't want to share his folks' wealth with me. So he shot his father in the back and stole his money, and his mother just wasted away with grief until she sort of willed herself into a grave. I was just a button then, twelve years old."

Carmen nodded, disbelief in her eyes. "How horrible."

Boon turned again and walked down the steps to his sorrel. "It *was* horrible," he admitted. "Now it's over at last."

Carmen came down into the street to stand before Boon once more.

"I have been told I am a bold woman, Boon. I don't wish to be, but I know once you leave this town I will not see you again.

I ask only one of two things. Hold me just for a moment so I will always remember you or let me leave this town with you. I have a feeling I will never meet a man like you again, and I would like the chance to know you better."

Taken aback, Boon gave the woman a look of frank appraisal. "You *are* a bold woman, Carmen, but like I said before, you have to ask some things or always wonder after the answer. I'm ridin' to San Antone. I'll leave in the morning. If you really are of a mind to, you're welcome to tag along, if you can set a horse. Maybe you can catch me up on a world without Rudd Cale's name in it."

Carmen smiled happily. "I can ride very well, Boon. You won't be sorry. And I, too, can cook those American pies."

Inside the Alamo Hotel, Anson Hipe stood at the swinging doors and watched Boon walk his sorrel down the street, Carmen at his side. Then he turned to face the room and let the shotgun hammers down. In answer to the questioning crowd, he explained who Boon was and the unforgivable crime of patricide Rudd Cale had committed to come by his riches and buy the town of Alamo.

Slowly, he walked over to the portrait of Santa Anna and the Alamo, now frameless and broken on the floor. He gazed at the body of big Rudd Cale, and a sad smile came unbidden to his lips.

"Boys, I guess Boon Cale just gave us the most powerful reminder ever about remembering the Alamo. Big Rudd Cale is dead. And it looks like Santa Anna just fell for the last time."

The following story, "You Might Have to Run," is true. All of the characters portrayed by name were real people, and each of them went through the events described.

In the late fall of 1862, Bear Hunter's band of Northwestern Shoshones pitched their winter camp in the Bear River Valley, along Beaver Creek, which was later renamed Battle Creek. This piece of land was then in Washington Territory, but later that same year became part of Idaho Territory.

The Northwestern Shoshone people had claimed this land for many years and spent their winters here in quiet and solitude, for to the Indian people winter time was a time of peace, not war.

Early in the morning of January 29, 1863, while the Shoshones were sleeping soundly in their bison robes, Colonel Patrick E. Connor's soldiers crossed over Bear River to confront the people in Bear Hunter's camp. The rest is a sad history…

YOU MIGHT
HAVE TO RUN

"You might have to run."

Those were the words of the chiefs to twelve-year-old Da Boo Zee and his friends when one of the elders caught them talking about being brave. A warrior's greatest strength lies not in his ability to fight, they said, but in his wisdom to know when to fight, and when to flee. A warrior must accept the fact that sometimes a man must run if his People are to survive.

The chief long knife, Colonel Patrick Connor, was coming to punish the wrongs of some wild Shoshones who had attacked some white people and stolen their horses. As far as anyone knew, those who had done this were not in this winter camp, so there was a good chance there was no danger. But on the other hand, word had spread among the people of the tribe: To Connor they were all just Indians. Perhaps he would not care that the real guilty braves were not here. Perhaps, to Connor, all must pay for the color of their skin.

But Da Boo Zee did not believe he would have to run, even though he could run like the wind if he chose to—his Shoshone name meant Cottontail Rabbit. These were good times for the Northwestern Shoshone—the *So-so-goi*, as they referred to themselves: Those-Who-Travel-On-Foot. The name no longer truly fit, for the Northwestern Shoshone had long since become mounted, but they were strong on tradition, and so they would always be the So-so-goi.

But regardless of their name, these were flush times for this band, Bear Hunter's people. Their warm tepees lined these banks of the Bear River and Beaver Creek and scattered throughout the flat valley floor. Pemmican and jerked meat and dried berries hung by the bag from the lodge poles. Many curly bison robes lay rolled in the lodges, robes that would warm the feet on those bitter cold nights ahead.

It was a time of celebration. Perhaps five or six hundred Shoshone were gathered here along the banks of the river and the creek, and smoke from the lodges filled the air. It was the time of the Warm Dance, when Shoshones gathered from all around to bring back the warm weather and to drive out the cold. There was dancing, singing, feasting. There was no horse racing now, for it was the cold time, time to conserve energy. But there was plenty of gambling and trading, and the men from the different clans eyed the young maidens with unhidden desire.

Not far away from this grand encampment lay the town the white man called Franklin. It was a small town, but there they had a place to trade for grains and breads, for cloth and beads and other finery. Da Boo Zee had been there, only once. It was not a place he wanted to go to again, for he was looked on there like an animal. A few of the people smiled at him, but even a boy of twelve knew when someone was smiling only to be polite. Those whites did not like him. They did not like his people. They tolerated them only because they felt guilty for moving them off their land.

Yet those whites did not really seem to believe this was the land of the Shoshone. They believed it was for them to take, to trample, to fence, farm... to ruin. The grass seed the Shoshone had relied upon for generations to make their bread, it was gone. The white man's cattle and horses grazed it over, knocked it down. It had little chance to grow tall, to turn to seed. The bison were gone, and the elk and deer nearly gone. The bighorn sheep, too, were dead. And in its place were these cattle and horses the Shoshones were not supposed to touch, as if instead they could survive on air alone, which would have been taken from them too, if there had been a way. The white man had come to Shoshone land, and in every sense had robbed their pantry, then replaced all of their food sources with food of their own, then prohibited the Shoshone people—the *Newe*—from touching it. Even to a small child like Da Boo Zee, the injustice seemed extreme, harsher almost than anything he could imagine.

But although Da Boo Zee heard his elders speak of these things, and he thought of them often, as he looked around him at the plentiful lodges, they were full of food and robes and weapons of every kind, and he knew deep down that someone was only trying to scare him.

His people were here on their own land. They had always been here and always would be. Their leader, Bear Hunter, was a great man, and he would let no harm come to them. He had many great warriors and chiefs, like San Pitch and Saguitch, and they would be sure that this camp remained a safe haven.

These past days the people of Pocatello and others had been here celebrating the time of the Warm Dance. Shoshones came from all over to meet here, to see old friends, to trade goods and trinkets. To tell the stories that by Newe custom could only be told in the winter, to laugh and dance and sing. Every story ended with the traditional Shoshone ending, "and the rat's tail fell off." Da Boo Zee used to laugh at it, but after a hundred stories that ended virtually the same—"the rat's tail fell off," or simply, "the rat's tail," the humor faded, and it became accepted as simply the way a man ended his stories. No one ever told him where the ending started. Maybe no one knew.

Da Boo Zee's belly was full. He watched other boys and girls running and playing in the snow, which by now was over a foot deep around the lodges, although within a hundred yards of the encampment, where the horses pawed for grass, it had been trampled down and in places was hard and crusty. Da Boo Zee was content to stay by his mother and sister and grandmother for the time being and watch the festivities, to feel the excitement in the air.

Yes, they had told Da Boo Zee and his friends they might have to run, if the Long Knives came. But the boy felt warm and loved here, and he was safe on Shoshone land.

Da Boo Zee knew that soon enough a large part of this camp would be empty. Only Bear Hunter's people would remain here, for Pocatello's band and the others had their own places to hold out for spring. They had their own valleys with game and with forage for their animals, although the boy couldn't imagine they were as fine as this one.

And so it was that in time a large part of the village lodges came down, and with travois poles attached to horses, and lodge poles tied together and lashed down, tepees rolled and ready to travel, Pocatello and the others took their people and made ready to go.

Da Boo Zee was there at his father's tepee when Pocatello came riding up on a chestnut mare and hopped down before them. Chief Bear Hunter had come over to pass part of the morning with them, and Pocatello had come to bid him farewell. But it was not a farewell of happiness. And for the first time Da Boo Zee came to know fear.

"So, you are ready to stop eating all of our food and go home," said Bear Hunter.

Pocatello almost smiled. It was the most humor he ever showed. "You make bad hosts," he said.

Bear Hunter grunted, then laughed. "Only because we wanted you to go home. When you are gone we will feast like a camp of chiefs."

Pocatello shot his eyes from Chief Bear Hunter to Da Boo Zee and his sister. "You will teach these young ones to laugh at us. Then we will have to separate you from your hair."

Bear Hunter's eyes were full of mirth, sparkling out above his full cheeks that crowded them like the two halves of an apple. He looked at the boy and his sister, then at their father.

"Ah, they laugh at you already, my friend!"

Pocatello grunted. By now Da Boo Zee knew he and Bear

Hunter were just having fun. But then the fun stopped.

"You are in a bad place, comrade," said Pocatello. "You know that."

Bear Hunter's cheeks tightened, and his sharp eyes scanned the horizon. "We spoke of it. The white men, they are crowding us close."

Pocatello pulled a piece of jerky from his pouch and ripped off a large chunk with his teeth, squinting toward the south. His eyes swung back around and met Bear Hunter's. "And they will crowd you closer. They are coming to take this valley, and they will keep coming. They will soon try to take my land as well. But I will not let them.

"Mark my words, my friend. This is your last year in this valley. Those springs—" he pointed toward a great cloud of steam rising up in the southwest, uphill from the camp— "they will not be for the Newe next harvest. The white man will be living there, bathing in them. I will tell you the truth, my brother; I am afraid for you."

Pocatello never spoke Bear Hunter's name. It was not polite and not good luck to speak a man's name to him too often.

Bear Hunter ground his teeth together. "Where else would you have us go? We have spoken of this before. The white man is coming. He does not go away. He wants it all. There is no place to go and find peace, to find food, where he will not come in time."

"But this time he is coming to kill you, my brother. If it is the long knife Connor coming, you will have to stand and fight. I am telling you this as your friend. I hope to see you next harvest. But I feel that we will not be together. You should come with us now. Give this place up. We will hold tight and fight together in my land. We will be strong together."

Bear Hunter shook his head. "No, my friend. This is my home. I have always wintered here. My people would not go. Saguitch. San Pitch. They like it here. This is where we are safe. For now."

Pocatello shrugged. "If you feel safe, then your medicine is telling you a different story than my medicine. I hope yours is stronger. This boy—" he reached out and put his hand on Da Boo Zee's shoulder— "you must let him live to be old enough to gain his warrior name. It is not right to let a boy die without a warrior name—still being called Cottontail Rabbit. You come with us. Or you stay here and be strong and make sure this boy lives. I will come back and let him hunt with me in a few harvests. He will be a great warrior."

Pocatello's eyes met the boy's and held. Da Boo Zee's chest swelled with pride. Yes, he would be a great warrior. And he would ride with Pocatello over the prairies and the valleys of this Shoshone land.

Pocatello rode out with his people that mid-morning, and Da Boo Zee watched him go. Pocatello was a fierce one. He hated the white man with everything inside him. He had bad memories of the whites, they said. He had reason to hate. But the boy looked at Pocatello and saw a dashing warrior with feathers flowing out of his hair, wearing fine buckskins and holding a sturdy lance that hung with eagle feathers. One day he would ride with Pocatello.

After Pocatello had gone, Bear Hunter came back over to Da Boo Zee's lodge. This time he came with Chief Saguitch. They sat and with pieces of bread for spoons ate the small bowls of venison soup the boy's mother dished up for them. Bear Hunter and Saguitch and Da Boo Zee's father sat for a long time and stared around them at the beautiful valley, white now with winter's shawl. On all sides were hills. On the south there was a plateau that rose up above the river and made a flat sharp line against the frosty blue sky. On the west, along with the giant plume of steam sent up by the hot springs, was a hill covered with juniper trees. On the west and north, a couple of miles away, were bald hills that looked smooth and soft with winter's snow, which had been falling for two and a half months now. Here in this valley was shelter, and the horses were able to find grass. On the ridges around them the snows were deep, sometimes as deep as a man's waist. They were safe here. No man would brave snows like that.

In his robe two weeks later, Da Boo Zee's dreams were filled with dancing and singing, but mixed in with the familiar faces he began to see other faces. White faces. They smiled at him, but they weren't happy smiles. They were evil smiles. Soon he began to see them all around, everywhere, and the more he looked the more the faces of his people disappeared and were replaced with the white faces. He awoke with sweat beaded on his forehead and looked around. It was pitch black in the tepee and smelled of musky buffalo hide and bodies, venison and sagebrush smoke. There was a sprinkling of stars in the sky he could see between the lodge poles.

When Da Boo Zee realized that no one else was awake, he lay very still and stared up at the lodgepoles. He thought about Pocatello and the words he had spoken. He also thought about what the elders had told him and the other boys. They might have to run. Run? Where could they run?

He tried to think of where he would go if he had to leave this valley. There was nowhere to run. The white man had pushed his people to the edge. They couldn't go into Crow country, or Sioux country, or Blackfoot country. They didn't mix so well with the people called Utes, even though they were supposed to be somehow related. So where did a people go once they no longer had a home? They could not just claim someone else's home as the white man had theirs.

The night was cold. He could feel his own breath coming frosty from his nostrils. He snuggled deeper in the robe.

At first it was only a far-off voice. Da Boo Zee had fallen back to sleep. He heard the distant voice, and it roused him from his slumber. The voice became an Indian voice that was yelling, angry, taunting. His father and mother were rousing. A gray light was in the sky; he could see it past the tops of the lodge poles.

All of them struggled to get dressed so they could go see what the commotion was about. The boy's father went outside first, and almost immediately he flashed back into the tepee.

"There are white men out there. The long knives." They called the soldier men long knives because of the long-bladed knives they carried hanging from their saddles, sometimes from their belts.

Fear leaped into the eyes of Da Boo Zee's mother. "Long knives? But why? Why do they come in the time of the deep snows?"

"There is trouble," his father said as he strapped a belt about his waist and secured his knife sheath and tomahawk. He picked up his bow and quiver and looked gravely at his wife, then at the two children. "Wait here and be ready." He looked at Da Boo Zee's grandmother. "You keep my family safe. Run to the river if you must run."

Then he was gone from the tepee. Da Boo Zee charged out after him, ignoring his father's and his grandmother's orders to stay. Warriors and women and children were stirring every-where, running with weapons in hand. The men ran out and formed a group toward the river bluffs, and beyond them, stand-ing with steam coming off their dripping wet clothes, were many long knives. More long knives than the boy had ever seen, or even dreamed of. Some of the warriors were yelling back and forth with the long knives. And while they were yelling more and more long knives were coming up from the river, their faces red from the cold. The sun was yet an hour away, and clouds hung low all around the valley, hiding the tops of the hills.

Without warning, a crackle of rifles started from among the Indian line, then became a deep roar. Da Boo Zee, in horror, saw long knives fall into the snow. The rifle fire was like thunder, and the snap of revolvers joined in. The warriors kept firing, but more and more long knives were gathering from the river, and looking toward the bluff Da Boo Zee could see more of them plunging down through the deep snow.

The line of warriors held for a time, but after the first burst of Shoshone fire, the long knives quickly rallied and began to return fire, and then the Shoshone line started to break. Some of them started running, and the long knives came after them. Da Boo Zee turned numbly and fell through the tepee door. His grandmother and mother and sister were frozen against one wall, but his mother, when she saw him fall, picked up a bow and arrows and threw open the door, crouching out and then standing up to look at what was happening.

People were crying now, running everywhere in confusion. Da Boo Zee came out to stand beside his mother. A horse screamed as it ran past. It was an Indian horse, rider-less. A woman fell by her tepee, and the boy saw blood on her face. Her small baby fell with her and started to cry, its voice soon drowned out by the gunfire and the screams of the horses, the roars of the angry, frightened men.

The People were begging for mercy, but there was no mercy that morning. A woman pleading with a soldier for her life was shot down by another man trotting by. A long knife horse ran past their tepee, its empty stirrups flapping against its sides.

Many of the people were running for the river. As Da Boo Zee spun in a circle, he could see those people and see others running for the creek and for the juniper covered hill to the west. Thinking of his father's words, the boy ran first for the river. He didn't think about his mother or his grandmother. He didn't think about what his elders had told him, that someday he might have to run. He didn't think. He only ran.

He jolted to a stop at the riverbank. In some places the river was three or four feet deep, and there was ice along its banks four feet wide. But some of his people were breaking the ice, wading out across the dark, steaming water, steaming not because it was warm but because it was not as cold as the frigid air. Soldiers began to gather along the banks, shooting at the people as they struggled across the water. One woman went under, still holding tight to her baby. They didn't come back up.

Da Boo Zee saw three women hiding beneath a bank in the willows. They were up to their waists in the freezing water and trying to be quiet so the soldiers wouldn't see them. One of them was a woman named Anzee Chee, and she held her little baby, her hand over its mouth. The baby was trying so hard to struggle free, and Anzee Chee, who was soaked with blood from chest and shoulder wounds, could hardly hold onto it. Da Boo Zee fell down into the willows and stared, wanting to run to the women because they were the nearest of his people.

Three soldiers came running along the bank, shooting the two or three people who made it to the other side of the river. They stopped right above the huddled women. Da Boo Zee saw the desperate look in Anzee Chee's eyes as her baby struggled free, and its wailing drew the attention of the men. She put the baby on her blanket and set it free into the river. As it came away from the bank, crying, the three soldiers shot at it until it disappeared into the dark current.

Looking up, Da Boo Zee saw two Indian horses galloping toward the river, and he recognized Saguitch and his son, Soguitch. Soguitch had a young Indian maiden on the pony behind him. It was the girl everyone in camp knew he intended to marry.

As the three raced away, shots from long knives' rifles made the girl fall from the horse, and they ran toward her, tearing at her clothes, as Saguitch and his son made it to the river and escaped across, disappearing in the gunsmoke.

You may have to run. Da Boo Zee heard the voice, and he ran, he ran like a deer, silently, for the other side of the camp, for the junipers.

Da Boo Zee saw his grandmother running for him, holding a buffalo robe. Her face was frozen with her lips pursed. She jarred to a stop in front of him and yelled, "Get down. Lie down!" The boy obeyed, as silent as the rabbit of his name.

He lay down among all the lifeless bodies on the hard, snowy ground that now was dark with blood. His grandmother lay down beside him and pulled the buffalo robe over them and told him not to move at all. Somehow he knew the rest of his family was dead.

The firing was sporadic now, the long knives carefully picking their targets. Time went by endlessly, and Da Boo Zee lay still on the icy ground the way he had been trained. He could feel his grandmother's warmth next to him, but the ground was soaking all of the heat out of his back. Long knives were yelling back and forth down by the river, up in the junipers, all around the camp and by the creek. Indian voices were now almost non-existent.

Hours passed. Or so it seemed. Da Boo Zee and his grandmother lay still, not daring to move. They could feel that sunlight had come to the valley, but it was a cold sunlight, the kind that does not send its warmth, only its light.

Suddenly, even with the ringing in his ears, Da Boo Zee became aware of the approaching sound of a soldier's boots, squeaking in the frozen powder snow. The sounds stopped by his head. Then blinding sunlight struck the boy as the buffalo robe was torn away. There stood a bearded, dark-haired man, staring at him from under shaggy brows. The man's lip twitched, and he glanced around him. Then he cocked his rifle and raised it, aiming at the boy's head.

For what seemed forever the man pointed the rifle at his head, and Da Boo Zee stared back at him, knowing he was about to die. Then the soldier lowered his rifle. He grimaced, then raised it again, still cocked, and closed one eye.

Again, his face changed, and he lowered the rifle. He scanned all around him at the bloody snow, at the sounds of the other men's voices. Some men were running, some were walking about, making the squeaking noises with their boots on the powdery snow. The blowing and snorting of horses could be heard above all but the scattered rifle shots came now only every twenty seconds or so.

The long knife raised his rifle one more time and pointed it at Da Boo Zee's forehead, and then a long shudder seemed to go through him as he was squeezing the trigger.

But he never squeezed it. His eyes seem to turn very sad, and then he just reached down and pulled the robe back over the boy, and Da Boo Zee heard him trudge away, crunching snow.

Da Boo Zee lay frozen to the ground, holding his breath. His grandmother sucked in a breath beside him. He thought of all the people he had seen run and die. He thought how this valley now belonged to the white people, how the Newe no longer had a winter home. He wondered how many of the People there were left. And he wondered if he would live out this day.

In his mind he could see the face of Bear Hunter, his chief. Bear Hunter looked at him with all the wisdom that shone out of his eyes, and he said, "You might have to run."

But this time not running had saved Da Boo Zee's life.

THE
RICHEST MAN
ON THE
MOUNTAIN

I told Mama I'd be rich within a year. She didn't believe me. Aunt Martha didn't believe me either. Even Jenny thought I was crazy. My own gal! Women. Goes to show what they know about a determined man.

From my viewpoint down here in this creek bottom, I can see little but the glitter of the largest vein of gold I have ever dreamed of. Well, in my mind's eye, anyway. But it's up there. I've seen it. And I'd bet forty good horses there isn't a man on the mountain who could hold a candle to the gold on my claim that's as common as road apples.

The wind howls like a forlorn woman. Air as cold as Jenny's feet swirls down into my shirt. Black clouds scud across the sky, some with long tails sweeping down, bluish against the canvas-white of clouds behind them. Snow is well on its way.

How much time do I have?

I look at the gold in my hand. I've been here in Colorado enough to see gold before, and lucky enough to be standing in the assayer's office when some prospector weighed his in. The nugget of rotted gold in my hand is as pure and gleaming yellow as any I've ever beheld. It couldn't be worth less than five hundred dollars. I clawed it off a ledge where it fell out of a vein in the side of the mountain—the biggest vein in all of Colorado, I'm wagering.

No telling how deep that vein runs, nor how wide it might get inside the mountain, but to judge it offhand, on the surface alone shines four or five thousand of the most beautiful dollars in God's creation.

"I won't get rich, huh, Mama?" I speak out loud, but there is nobody to hear me.

Would she find out now! Her boy isn't as worthless as folks made out. They had all laughed—menfolk too. Ab Jeeters, the bully of my childhood, had jeered and told me not only was I *not* going to get rich, but while I was gone he was going to steal my Jenny. Truth told, I'm still mad at her anyway, since she had no more belief in me than in a shredded Confederate dollar. Still, I don't want to lose her—especially not to Ab, a man I'd still like to give back the gift of all the bloody noses he ever gave me in one pretty package.

I'm telling this to the wind, since she is the only one here to hear me—her and the birds I see darting from branch to branch at the corner of my vision. I'm the richest man on this mountain! And here's how this came to be . . .

I woke up on day three hundred sixty-four of my absence from Connecticut with an empty belly and ragged clothes. My boots were in tatters, and winter snapping at my heels. I had finally found me a rich creek. Panning it in my bare feet, so I wouldn't ruin what remained of the fragments of my boots, I got me a stake. Maybe two-hundred fifty in dust. Nothing but dust. Not even one smooth nugget. A long ways from its mother source, to be sure. Too far to think I had found me a mine. But at least I could buy some food, and maybe some lumber, and build a sluice.

I saddled up my bob-tail mule—yeah, some corral mates had harassed him and chewed his tail near in two, picked on just like his master—and I headed into town to buy supplies.

That's when I met up with local thug Jig Hawley and five of

his men. Pointing a lot of guns around, they joked about taking my clothes, but they didn't. They only degraded me some and then stole my mule and gold and left me alone and afoot.

I had nothing left, and winter kissing my neck. Tomorrow would be a year since I left home. I wasn't rich. I was dead-broke. I would have no Jenny, no respect from Mama or my other relatives. No nothing. I was the exact failure they all claimed.

Well, they would never know. That's what I was thinking. They could just wonder whatever happened to their dreamer. I found this cliff, and I started climbing, and I have no shame in telling you I meant to jump from the top of all hundred feet of that rock into this same creek and take my life. That's what I was down to.

So I got almost to the very top, all set to jump, and as I pulled myself over the rim, there gleamed the most beautiful sight in my whole life—and that includes my fickle Jenny. Thousands of dollars in pure gold, with nothing to do but pick it from the cliff and haul it out.

I reached for that biggest chunk, a good three-pound chunk of mostly gold with just a little bit of quartz mixed in. It just lay there on the ledge! I grabbed it up, but before I knew it my feet slipped.

I found myself plummeting through the air. I landed in this shallow creek, on my back, and now, other than my head and my arms, I can't move. I've been trying.

Winter coming, me alone in a half-freezing creek, and with probably a million-dollar claim just waiting to be staked. Chances are good, to judge by the sky, all that gold will be covered in snow by tomorrow morning. Maybe I will be too.

With a grim, weak smile, I let the gold roll off my fingers into the depths of a watery hole along the side of the big boulder I had landed close to. Even though I lie in shallow water, maybe no more than five inches deep, that hole is more like a foot or two. Probably no one but the trout will ever see that gold again.

I find myself wishing I could see my mama right now, and

Aunt Martha. And Jenny. I would look them all in the eyes and remind them what I had said before I left. I would be rich within a year. And now my claim has come true.

Tomorrow will be a year since I left home, and today I have become the richest man on the mountain—with gold to throw away.

AUTHOR'S
NOTE

If you have enjoyed these stories, as I have enjoyed writing them for you, please feel free to drop me a line at: kirby@kirbyjonas. com.

While I cannot guarantee to write future stories according to my readers' wishes, it is very important to me to hear what my readers think, and if they are looking for certain kinds of stories, either tales of the Old West or other kinds of stories. Please feel free to give me your comments. I strive to write back to each and every email I get from my readers.

Thank you.

Books by Kirby Jonas

Season of the Vigilante Book I (1994)
Season of the Vigilante Book II (1996)
The Dansing Star (1997)
Death of an Eagle (1998)
Legend of the Tumbleweed (1999)
Lady Winchester (2000)
The Devil's Blood (2001) (Combination of Season of the Vigilante books)
Yaqui Gold (2003) (co-author Clint "Cheyenne" Walker)
The Secret of Two Hawks (2012)
Knight of the Ribbons (2013)
Drygulch to Destiny (2014)
Samuel's Angel (2015)
The Night of my Hanging (and other stories) (2015)

LEGENDS WEST SERIES
Disciples of the Wind (2005) (co-author Jamie Jonas)
Reapers of the Wind (2006) (co-author Jamie Jonas)

LEHI'S DREAM SERIES
Nephi Was My Friend (2015)
The Faith of a Man (2015)
A Land Called Bountiful (2015)
Shores of Promise (forthcoming 2016)
Altar of the Wilderness (forthcoming 2016)

BOOKS ON AUDIO

Narrated by James Drury, "The Virginian"
Published by Books in Motion (www.booksinmotion.com)
Available through the author at www.kirbyjonas.com

The Dansing Star
Death of an Eagle
Legend of the Tumbleweed
Lady Winchester

Yaqui Gold, narrated by Gene Engene
The Secret of Two Hawks, narrated by Kevin Foley
(Winner, 2010 Spur Award from Western Writers of America,
"Best Western Audiobook")
Knight of the Ribbons, narrated by Rusty Nelson

To order books, go to www.kirbyjonas.com or write to:

Howling Wolf Publishing
1611 City Creek Road
Pocatello ID 83204

Or send email to: kirby@kirbyjonas.com